BUILD

UNIVERSES

GW00673793

Clare Island's
Dark Secret

Roddy O'Sullivan

ISBN 979-12-201-2988-6
First edition: October 2022

Clare Island's Dark Secret

PROLOGUE

Scattered along Ireland's west coast lie long-neglected ruins of prehistoric fortresses and burial places. Because all written evidence concerning the builders of these impressive structures – the Fomorians – has been either destroyed or lost, only stories and myths survive. Whereas local folklore suggests that these people originated from Ancient Greece, we may never learn why they disappeared. Notable athletes and sailors, they are credited with inventing Irish music and Gaelic games. Until recently, the Fomorians have remained a question mark on the pages of Irish history for over three thousand years.

Ancient Historic Locations Associated with
The Fomorians

Chapter 1

"He's well late," said Zara Singh, checking her mobile. "No way should it take five hours to get here from Dublin airport."

"He had to collect all that household stuff," said Shane Donnegan.

"Maybe he's been abducted by aliens?" sniped Finbar (Tubs) McAuley, doing his best to keep a straight face.

Lounging on the balcony of St Columbanus School, Shane and his two friends were awaiting the arrival of Shane's dad, who'd earlier flown in from Brisbane to belatedly celebrate his son's birthday. The trio had long lost interest in watching the end-of-term stream of vehicles ferrying away pupils and staff. Below, the main hall was stacked with trunks, sports gear and musical instruments; everyone seemed to have laptops clutched under their arms and be dragging suitcases or holdalls, many leaking unwashed socks and underwear. Those trying to manoeuvre bicycles through the crowd were loudly abused or worse. The feeling of freedom and release was everywhere.

"So who lives in your Granddad's cottage?" said Zara. "Since he died, I mean."

"A neighbour looks after the place... I think."

"You think?" cried Tubs in mock alarm. "Are you tellin' me you've invited us to spend a holiday with rats and creepy crawlies?"

When the laughter subsided, Shane said, "Granddad's should be in good nick. Anyway, Dad's a DIY freak; he'll have everything up and running in no time and..." He leapt to his feet. "Here he comes."

Crunching up the driveway from the main gates, the red and white VW campervan trailed a haze of dust. Shane recognised his Manchester United flag draped across the side window which partially hid boxes that sprouted everything from household tools to cluttered bags of bed linen and kitcheny stuff.

"Hey, nice ride." Zara beamed.

"As a birthday treat he said he'd hire something with loads of room. Let's hoick our gear downstairs."

Shane led the way through the deserted dormitories, aware of just how empty the school felt with even the cooks and cleaners gone. The pong of sweaty PE kit and unwashed linen was also absent; everywhere smelt of air freshener and floor polish.

Father and son met outside in the car park. They hugged each other in silence, and after some seconds broke apart, still regarding each other with unconcealed affection.

"How's everything going, son?" said Mr Donnegan.

"Great, Dad." Shane punched him playfully. "How's the leg coming along?"

"Right as rain, plaster came off on Monday." Realising Shane's friends were standing to attention close by, Mr Donnegan extended his hand. "You must be the famous Zara? I've heard a lot about you."

"Hi, Mr Donnegan."

"And you, I take it – are Finbar McAuley, eh? Put it there."

"Forget the Finbar bit, Mr D," said Tubs. "Everyone calls me Tubs on account of my…" He winked and pointed to his ample waistline, "…heavy bones! Is it true we'll be sleepin' in your barn with sheep and cows?"

Mr Donnegan chuckled. "I can see who the joker of this group is. No, Finbar, er, Tubs, a friend keeps an eye on the house. Are you guys all in the same year?"

Zara pointed at Tubs. "The Professor there is head of the scholarship group. The three of us are day pupils; fifth class."

"Anyway, sorry I'm so late," said Mr Donnegan, "I got delayed saying hello to my Uncle Lionel and Aunt Agnes. Shane lives with them while I slave my life away in Brisbane and…"

"…We know them well, Mr D," interrupted Tubs, passing around a bag of Gummy Bears.

Zara smiled and rolled her eyes, "I'm still trying to teach Lionel how to make classical music playlists on Spotify."

Mr Donnegan checked his watch. "I want to make Granddad's place before dark to get everything ship-shape. Best load your stuff on board."

"Come on then," cried Shane with a loud yee-haw, heading for the camper.

Mr Donnegan watched the trio race down the incline with their bags, Tubs already lagging behind. "Can't get over how that son of mine has sprouted," he muttered, scratching his head. "I barely recognise him."

***

After ten minutes the camper left the main road and took the meandering costal route through small rural villages, past stacks of drying turf, all set against the wide landscape of rolling hills and desolate moorland. Since enrolling at St Columbanus, Shane had seen little of the surrounding countryside, so he was enjoying the journey more than he'd expected to. The narrow, unfrequented road was lined by low stone walls and unkempt hedgerows, whose trees were stunted and bent by the fierce Atlantic winds.

Mr Donnegan adjusted the driving mirror and called over his shoulder, "Everyone comfy back there?"

"Yes," they chorused.

Zara held her tablet aloft. "Does your place have wifi, Mr Donnegan?"

"Afraid not, Zara; even the mobile signal can be dodgy this far west. Hey, Shane, how did your first term go?"

Shane continued to gaze through the window. "Fine, Dad."

"These roads are certainly not fine," grumbled Mr Donnegan, braking to avoid a sheep crossing the road. "There's hardly enough room for two wheelbarrows to pass each other, never mind cars."

"How far away is the sea from the house, Mr Donnegan?"

"Right on the doorstep, Zara."

Shane pointed as they passed through a small village. "Hey, I didn't realise it was forty k's to Granddad's."

Mr Donnegan turned sharply. "That signpost was in Irish; have you learnt Gaelic already?"

"Hey, Mr D, what about your one-and-only son winnin' the under-19 swimmin' competition?"

"Under-19? But Shane's barely fourteen, he..."

"...Well, he spaghettified everyone, includin' the school champ."

Zara rested her elbow on the back of the driver's seat and bent close to Mr Donnegan's ear. "And that's not all," she whispered conspiratorially. "Your boy also broke the school record!"

"What?" gasped Mr Donnegan, adjusting the rear view mirror to focus on Shane's face.

"...No big deal, Dad; a race is only a race and..."

"...Oy, Mr D, any more dark-horse swimmers in the family? Yourself maybe?"

Wrinkles of mirth appeared around Mr Donnegan's blue eyes. "The Donnegans are world beaters at doing the brick stroke, Finbar – straight to the bottom! Shane didn't swim that much during his stay in Oz, there's no way he could win…" He chuckled. "So pull the other one; you lot must think I was born yesterday!"

"It's gospel, Mr D," said Tubs emphatically.

Without warning Mr Donnegan braked, cut the engine and stared sightlessly down the deserted road. "Is all this stuff on the level, Shane?" he asked, turning around from the driver's seat.

"Why all the fuss, Dad?" said Shane shrugging his shoulders.

Mr Donnegan muttered, "Finnoula, would've been real proud of you, son."

Zara frowned. "Who's Finnoula?"

Mr Donnegan rubbed the side of his cheek. "Shane's mother, God rest her soul; she… she passed away before Shane and me emigrated, when he was only a nipper..." Trying to sound upbeat, he restarted the engine. "Understanding Irish *and* breaking swimming records? Now I've heard everything."

Chapter 2

Shane jumped from the still-moving campervan as it slowly braked to a standstill. Swallows flitted along Granddad's tree-lined driveway; the tangles of dense bushes were alive with birdsong. Magnetically drawn to the rear of the house by the smell and sound of the ocean, he waved Tubs and Zara to follow as he sprinted towards the bottom of the long, sloping garden and clambered on top of the wall overlooking the sea.

Everything is so blue, he thought, *water, sky, even the hills look blue. Not another house to be seen. I could almost leap into the water...*

Ringed by a copse of pine trees and uneven walls, Granddad's whitewashed homestead sat alone at the end of a promontory that jutted into the estuary, its overgrown gardens ablaze with wildflowers, weeds and briars. Hearing a series of coughing barks, Shane craned over the wall to see three large animals belly-flopping across the shingle.

"Look," he shouted, pointing at the seals disappearing into the sea.

To his left and right, the adjacent grassy strips of land extending into the bay reminded him of the outstretched fingers of some giant's hand. Volcano-shaped St Patrick's Mountain filled the foreground, its tiny church gleaming whitely on the summit. *That hazy bulk on the horizon must be Clare Island...*

"What do you reckon, guys?" said Mr Donnegan, who'd arrived from behind and was watching the wonderment shining in their eyes.

"Great place, Dad…"

"…Magic, Mr D."

"It's kind of awesome," Zara had to concede.

"You three unpack," came Mr Donnegan's no-nonsense command. "And that means now. I'll see about getting this place fit to sleep in."

Shane surveyed the exterior of the house. What was left of the paint was bubbled with damp and the windows hadn't seen a cloth for years. Weeds sprouted from the gutters; moss mottled the walls. Sandblasted by the elements, the oaken front door was sound, although dotted with lichen. He looked up to see the weather-beaten carving of a single eye that stared outwards from the lintel and began massaging his forehead as if trying to shift some stinging discomfort. He tingled with a weird sensation of having experienced the identical situation before, somewhere in the buried past, in some prior time or existence. *I've never been here before yet everything feels so familiar... this place means something to me...* He shook his head to clear his thoughts.

"What gives with that wooden eye, Dad?" he asked.

"Where?"

"That carving over the door; it reminds me of something..."

Fingering his bunch of keys, Mr Donnegan muttered, "That's been there since long before my Dad's time."

Shane shouldered open the door and felt oddly disappointed when it failed to creak ominously. Comprising a traditional Irish cottage attached to a converted stable, Granddad's place was far more spacious than he'd expected. Only a stuffed squirrel and a mottled oil painting decorated the walls; the sparse furniture was covered in sheets. Everywhere smelt of mildew and mouse droppings and each footstep released spats of powdery dirt. The house threw their voices back, hollow and unfamiliar. For some reason he couldn't explain, Shane felt at home.

"Dry as the desert," said Mr Donnegan, shielding his nose and making humming noises of approval. "Open all the windows to air the place. Then we'll get stuck in."

Getting stuck in meant warp-speed unpacking followed by scrubbing and sweeping every square centimetre of the cottage. Even Tubs, who'd elevated the dodging of housework to an art form, put his everything into it.

After two hours, the friends stood with arms round each other in the living room, finally able to see through windows free of grime and cobwebs.

"Any chance of somethin´ to eat, Mr D?" bleated Tubs.

"He's hungry again," said Zara.

Shane cupped his hands and hollered, "Any tucker, Dad?"

A muffled voice came from the nearby cubbyhole. "Those crisps and biscuits should keep you going." Carrying a toolbox, sooty-faced Mr Donnegan struggled through the narrow aperture into the room. "I'll shortly nip into the village for supplies but unless I get this Stone Age fuse box to work we'll be rubbing sticks to light a fire. Hey; how about collecting some mussels; maybe catch a fish for supper? The rods are rigged. Take that bucket and plastic bag. Off with you."

Needing no second invitation, Tubs was already stuffing his mouth and pockets. "A great welcome," he said mutinously but keeping his voice low. "Catch your own food or starve!"

Zara light-heartedly shouldered him. "Stop moaning and get your wellies on."

***

The mussel beds lay exposed by the receding tide so the rocks were festooned with clusters of the shellfish. Their pail was soon overflowing. Shane's attention was initially taken by three baby flatfish sinking to the bottom of the nearby tidal pool, camouflaging their brown bodies beneath layers of sand. He scaled the adjacent outcrop of boulders and pointed towards the dark carpet of shells that littered the seabed. "What are they, Tubs?"

"Oysters, I reckon."

"I could easily dive for them, except…"

"…Cept what?"

"I've no swimming gear."

Zara laughed into her palm. "Anyone stopping you swimming in your pants?"

"He doesn't want us to see his skid marks."

Stripped to his underpants, Shane pushed into the cold water. With the plastic bag dangling from his arm he was abreast of the oyster beds in three strokes and inhaling deeply, plunged below, hardly making a ripple.

From a flat overhanging boulder, Tubs and Zara watched him explore the seabed, languidly collecting shellfish, his body showing whitely as he drifted above the oysters. Suddenly he changed direction and with a dolphinlike swirl, accelerated into gloomier, deeper water.

A little later, Zara let out a sudden gasp. Not only had Shane disappeared from sight but he'd been underwater for some considerable time. She checked the display on her phone. "He's been down for over three minutes," she cried. "No one can stay underwater for that long."

Tubs was also on his feet, shielding his eyes, squinting into the depths, then switching his attention further out to sea.

"Somethin' must've happened…"

Fifty metres from shore Shane's dark mop and raised fist broke the calm surface. "Ahoy," he hollered. "The ship's coming ashore."

Using a powerful backstroke, he propelled himself shoreward and when alongside Tubs and Zara, theatrically spewed a long arc of seawater in their direction. In the same movement he displayed the bag dangling from his wrist, laden with oysters.

"What happened to you?" cried Zara as he jettisoned the shellfish and clambered onto the rocks.

"Nothing. I just went for a swim. What about those monster oysters?"

"Look," Zara said, her eyes widening as she pointed at Shane's torso. "You're as dry as a bone…"

Tubs' artificial country-yokel accent cut in. "Come 'ere; I be thinkin' that lad's skin's hydrophobic."

Shane smiled. *Hydrophobic? Whatever that means! No wonder the teachers call him the Professor; he spouts more jawbreakers than a dictionary.*

"Be serious," cried Zara. "Shane's skin is seriously weird – look – water doesn't stick to it. Like it does me. I've never seen anything like that..."

"…Stop fussing, Zara, my skin dries really quickly, that's all. Grab the rods."

Having stashed the shellfish into a crevice above the tide and out of reach of the gulls, Shane led them away from the rocks, sending wading birds running twinkling ahead on the hard, wet shoreline. The beach was bare of all footprints except for the birds' tripod indentations. *They're so delicate and restless; always on the go, like most living things in nature…*

"Come back to earth, Mr Swimmer Man," said Zara, a challenge in her eyes. "Show us how it's done."

On retrieving his initial cast, Shane's rod arced like an overstrung bow and the reel screamed as something big took the bait and sped into the open Atlantic. *Yippee! A take on my first cast – my luck is in.* Teeth clenched, he sank his heels into the sand, rod tip upright. Encouraged by the others' shouts of advice, he eventually succeeded in turning the fish towards the shore but it abruptly changed tack and headed back towards the open ocean.

For ten minutes the contest continued – Shane would later admit it seemed like ten hours – before the fish began to tire. Without warning, the calm surface of the ocean broke open and an elongated silver shape emerged, rising high above the water. It seemed to hang momentarily before falling with a splash that drove the spray up high and white.

"Get a load of that," gasped Tubs.

Shane had stopped breathing, fearful the bait might come free at any moment. Approaching the shore and feeling the rise in temperature, the fish again exploded into the air but Shane knew its strength was ebbing fast. Keeping the line taut, he waded knee deep into the tide and carefully manoeuvring the fish into the shallows, gently drew it on to the beach at the very moment the hook came free. In silence they regarded its jaws opening and closing spasmodically.

"What is it?" asked Shane softly.

"Seabass by my reckonin'. Five kilo if it's an ounce."

"Wow."

On cue, the boys high-fived. Then Tubs pantomimed playing a violin as he sang crazily,

"We are the men, we are the men,
We are the world's best fishermen."

"What about fisher girls?" cried Zara indignantly.

"Spare me, oh, Lord," said Tubs, looking to the heavens. "OK, OK, fisher girls as well."

Shane wasn't listening. "It's a shame to kill a thing as beautiful as this. We're not his enemies or anything?"

"What's eatin' you? You've just caught the biggest whopper in the business."

Shane used both hands to carefully raise the bass from the sand and carry it towards the water.

"What are you doin'?" yelled Tubs.

"I'm putting him back."

"*What?*"

"But, Shane," cried Zara, "he's big enough to feed us for a week."

Shane first immersed the grey head then pointed the fish's body to the open sea. He released his hold. "Bye, old fella," he whispered.

For two seconds the long shadow hung motionless in the tide, then with an almost imperceptible swirl of its tail, edged into deeper water and with a sudden spurt, vanished.

Zara shook her head. "What was all that about, Tubs?"

"He's a nutter."

"Grab the shellfish, you two," said Shane, "let's head back."

To Shane the cottage seemed more visible in the gathering twilight. The mutinous brambles had been levelled and the hedges trimmed. A fire threw soft shadows over the living room and across the lawn that sloped down to the shoreline. The mouth-watering aroma of frying food wafting from the kitchen reminded Shane of just how ravenous they were.

"Mussels and oysters," cried Mr Donnegan, appearing in the doorway. Carrying their haul inside he asked, "Did you catch anything with fins?"

"The anglin' champion over there caught the biggest bass the world has ever seen, Mr D."

"Where is it?"

"Your one and only livin' son put it back."

Seeing Shane's clouded expression, Mr Donnegan changed the subject. "Hey, those oysters are the size of tennis balls. I'll have a feast knocked up in no time. Look behind, Shane, I've prepared a little surprise for you." A large chocolate cake with marzipan, icing and candles, sat in the middle of the table. "Sorry I couldn't make it over in time, so belated happy birthday, son."

"Great, Dad, thanks, you shouldn't have bothered; Aunt Agnes and Uncle Lionel already threw a small party for me."

"That cake looks delish, Mr D."

"Oy, greedy guts!" cried Zara, pulling Tubs aside. "Get your claws off that icing."

Mr Donnegan clapped his hands. "How about you lot setting the table? Tonight we eat by candlelight."

***

After the meal, they moved into the garden, each carrying a helping of birthday cake. Tubs' plate was heavily laden. The Milky Way blazed across the sky, brighter than Shane had ever remembered it. A strange hush hung in the air as he watched small bats flit in and out of the pines like fluttering flakes of erratic darkness. Slowly, from behind the mountain, the full moon, resembling a surreal Christmas tree decoration, transformed the sea into a shimmering silver sheet. The day had been great – Shane just wished it would go on forever. He wanted to somehow touch the whole landscape in front because it was too wide to take in through his eyes alone.

"Dad, where to tomorrow?"

"Inisturk."

"What's wrong with Clare Island, Mr D?" asked Tubs. "It's much nearer and the fishin's great."

Mr Donnegan didn't answer, just scratched his head.

"What's botherin' you about Clare Island, Mr D?" continued Tubs.

"Maybe because I can still hear my mother threatening to imprison me in the caves below the island if I don't finish my cabbage. Silly, but there you are..."

"...But Mr Donnegan," said Zara. "You said *we* could choose our fishing spot for helping you clean up the place."

"OK, then, Clare Island it is. Remember though, no gaming allowed; this is a fresh air holiday, right?"

The three exchanged dubious glances then nodded.

In the bay below, Shane's attention was caught by something breaking the surface, sending ripples of phosphorescence into the depths. As the grass stirred faintly in the breeze, he watched his friends, as relaxed as cats while his father contentedly sipped from a glass. The incoming tide laced brilliant silver through the glistening dark of the mudflats. Far out on the sandbanks, a bird called with a long melancholy series of falling tones.

Nothing could spoil this.

Chapter 3

Having tussled with the duvet for ages, Shane finally accepted he couldn't sleep. *It must be the holiday excitement zinging in my veins.*

Zara was in the adjoining room. Tubs, snoring like a horse in the upper bunk, wasn't making matters any easier. *I wish he'd keep quiet.*

He slung the duvet aside and headed off to the attic, intending to plonk himself down somewhere and maybe read until he was ready to finally nod off. White moonlight showed the way as he moved barefoot along the corridor. Then came the unnerving thought – how come he knew the place so well?

He glanced over his shoulder. *Funny how ghosts and stuff never give you the jitters in daylight; different kettle of fish when it's dark. The floor is shimmering, as if the floorboards are momentarily liquefying then solidifying again…*

"Get a grip on yourself," he heard himself croak.

He whipped round. The walls and ceiling were now behaving like the floor. With a dreadful clarity, he instinctively knew where his footsteps were taking him. Although he couldn't yet see it, he knew *that* door waited for him.

He stiffened.

That smell.

Indistinct at first but now growing in intensity, it reeked of mould and damp – the stench of wetted human ashes! A tremor shot through his body. The murky entrance lay ahead, shrouded in swirling shadows. He wanted to turn away but some powerful force was driving him remorselessly onwards.

He again recognised the same indistinct painting of an eye that dominated the door's central panels. The same faded words; the same carvings of interconnecting circles, each in identical groups of three. Claustrophobia saturated his senses as the two stone sculptures buttressing the doorway began to move of their own volition. With arms folded and two horns protruding from each skull, their hollowed eyes were full of inky emptiness. He saw their mouths open and emit hoarse garbled words. His hand shot to his mouth; he understood what they were saying!

Beneath his feet the floor continued to buckle and distort with every step he took.

Run! He commanded himself.

He plunged back along the passageway, his muscles straining and pulling against the blackness. After his initial spurt, he realised it was towards the door he was running, not away from it! Gasping, he was face to face with the entrance. A group of toga-clad men stood in the distance, shouting at him. The hair on the back of his neck was erect. There was no escaping whatever waited on the other side of the door but he *knew* that it was the living embodiment of all his childhood fears, making every cell in his body quail with a feeling of flesh-crawling, impending doom. He had no choice but to advance and confront his fate. Terror, not courage, was impelling him into the open mouth of the...

Silently screaming into wakefulness, he wrestled with the duvet, then kicked it aside. His gasps were the only sounds in the room.

Tubs shook him again. "Wakey, wakey!" he said, concern in his voice. "It's only a dream."

Shane's wide eyes scanned the walls, then the sunlit garden outside, before he flopped back into the pillow, trying to regulate his breathing. "It's the same nightmare,

Tubs, and it always takes place somewhere far away. This time it was *here*. Upstairs."

Tubs frowned. "Shane... there *is* no upstairs."

Shane grabbed Tubs' pyjama front. "There was this door, with something *so* horrible behind it, guarded by two statues that... spoke to me..." He licked his dry lips.

"Sayin' what?"

"Some weird stuff; they called me an intruder..."

Tubs was nibbling his nails. "Shane, there's somethin' whacko going on in your head... you were babblin' nonsense words..."

"...Maybe it has something to do with that the programme; remember, everyone was speaking Ancient Greek and..."

"...That film was so borin' I fell asleep." Tubs continued to stare at Shane.

In the ensuing silence it was obvious from their flummoxed expressions that each was as bewildered as the other.

Zara appeared in the doorway. "Rise and shine, campers," she called cheerfully. "Breakfast on Clare Island. We're ready to cast off."

Tubs stood up, his face deadly serious. "How would you say in Ancient Greek," he asked, "*I'm always dreamin' weirdo dreams*?" Giving his kicked-piglet laugh, he skipped out the door.

***

Clare Island basked in the early morning sunshine. Propped against a rock with hands behind his head, Shane lay close to the walls of the deserted lighthouse. Perched high and dominating the scattering of inshore islands, it appeared unnaturally white against the surrounding blue.

Zara and Tubs were collecting driftwood. A column of smoke rose from the campfire close to where Mr Donnegan had tethered *Faith*, the rented blue and white twenty-footer. Zara's shadow fell across Shane's sprawled body.

"Oy," she said, hands on hips. "Everyone is helping out. Even Tubs."

Shielding his face from the sun with an upturned palm, Shane groaned, "I didn't sleep great, Zara. I'll do the washing up. Promise."

"Help out or no breakfast."

"But…"

"…No buts. Food's ready," she said, walking away.

Shane arrived to find Tubs and Mr Donnegan squatting by the campfire, holding out their plates as Zara divvied out wodges of food.

"Mr Donnegan," she said, "ever see such a lazy blob as your son?"

Silently scanning the horizon, Mr Donnegan said, "The weather forecast guaranteed sunshine, I'm not so sure."

"Weather forecasting is a bit of a joke, Dad. Those guys are paid good money even when they give out wrong forecasts..."

"…I wouldn't want *Faith* to get caught in a storm."

"Worriers," said Zara.

Mr Donnegan stretched himself out on the grass and cleared his throat. "Ireland's earliest settlers lived on this here island, way before Noah and his Ark. Right where we're parked today, Fomorians, they were called. *Fo* is the Irish word for under and *moire* means the sea, so they were supposedly *undersea dwellers*. Strange folk, by all accounts."

"Sounds like a cool story," said Zara, hugging her knees.

Mr Donnegan set down the smoke-tasting tea. "They say the island was some sort of ancient site where…"

"…Look, gannets," interrupted Tubs, pointing at the pair of large white birds flying offshore.

"You should know," said Zara sweetly. "You eat like one."

"I hear thunder, Dad," cut in Shane, biting his lip.

The distant rumble had Mr Donnegan on his feet. Flinging away his tea he ordered, "You lads douse that fire; Zara, stand by to loosen the ropes. Don your life-jackets. We've got to make the harbour before that storm breaks. Weather bloody forecasters."

As the three friends scrambled aboard, Mr Donnegan switched on *Faith's* engine which immediately growled into life.

Really glad that started thought Shane as he watched the wake of bubbles spill out behind the accelerating boat.

***

Dwarfed by the ominously darkening sky, *Faith* motored at half throttle. A forked lance of brilliance flashed from the heavens, followed by an abrupt crack of thunder that hit Shane's eardrums like a fist. Face shining with a mixture of seawater and rain, he huddled behind the windshield, protected from the biting rain that struck like handfuls of grit. The wind's moan had changed to a high-pitched shriek.

"Those waves are gettin' bigger, Mr D," called Tubs from inside the cabin, his words distorted by the wind.

"Wimp," shouted Zara, grasping the handrail.

As the sea pushed them towards the shelter of the inner bay, Shane watched the storm crisscross the swell in unpredictable gusts of ferocity, making it necessary for the boat to proceed at a crawling pace. *Hit one of those waves at the wrong angle and we'll be crab food within minutes – even with lifejackets on. The wind is from the west at thirty knots. The boat's speed is....*

"Shane. Shane! Snap out of it!"

Shane stared into Zara's troubled eyes, aware that she was shaking him and shouting at the same time. "What are you jabbering about, Shane? It sounds like Greek. We're nearly ashore!"

Tubs caught Shane by the shoulder. "You looked like you were in a trance. You certainly weren't on this planet, that's for sure."

Shane shook his head. Normally visible for miles on a clear day, he could just about make out Clare Island's only hotel as *Faith* continued to judder against the inside of the harbour wall. Although screened from the storm, the boat still bucked violently. Mr Donnegan, engrossed with lashing *Faith* to the pier, was unaware of just how strangely Shane had behaved in the stern.

"Don't forget your mobile, Shane," he shouted, securing the last of the mooring ropes.

Followed by the others, Shane was first up the steps of the jetty. In the diminishing light, they dragged themselves up the hill, bent double against the wind. The hotel door almost blew open as they struggled to get inside.

The bustling interior was crammed. Steaming plates of stew and the log fire almost neutralised the reek of drying clothes and sweaty bodies. Through the condensation on the windows and the rivulets of cascading rain, Shane watched the trees swaying dementedly outside and snuggled closer to the fire, still trying to make sense of what Zara and Tubs had said to him…

***

Half an hour later, the storm abated as quickly as it had risen and shafts of sunlight began to lance through the scudding clouds. As the hotel bar became a great desert of boredom, Shane eyed the door like a caged tiger.

"It's time for us to explore, Dad."

"Too many people yakkin', if you ask me, Mr D. Should've brought my tablet."

Releasing an exaggerated sigh, Zara added, "I'd rather fold bedclothes all afternoon than hang around this place."

Mr Donnegan jabbed his watch. "Make sure you're back here on the dot of five. We mustn't miss the homeward tide."

Relieved to be out in the open, Shane led the way down the deserted pathway leading to the sea. The land was healing itself after the cloudburst; the yellow gorse appearing unnaturally bright against the green while the smell of recent wetness puffed from the fields.

In the slanting sunlight the almost hidden inlet caught Shane's fancy. The whole extent of the short beach was clear and glistening. Although the wind had dropped, the ocean was still angry, blustering into the rocky recesses and sweeping violently along the cliffs.

"What's that…" began Zara.

Her voice tailed off. Shane and Tubs, following her line of sight came to a standstill. Below, a figure was immersed up to the waist, slowly emerging from the sea.

Facing away from the trio, it was dragging something bulky from the surf with a rope.

"What's he up to?" whispered Shane.

"He's pullin' somethin' heavy; a box of fish?"

"Maybe he's fallen out of a boat or something…"

Shane knew that neither explanation sounded remotely adequate.

The three continued to advance warily down the incline to the beach, gaping at the still-reversing figure. Shane felt his apprehension increase as the man's abnormally tall build became obvious. There was also something unsettling about the broad shoulders and long scraggly hair that made his stomach churn. Except for a flimsy loincloth, the man was naked and without warning, he swung round.

"Oh, my God," gasped Zara, hand shooting to her mouth.

What glared unblinkingly at them was human in every respect except one. The being had only one eye – an abnormally large one – set in the middle of its forehead.

Chapter 4

Nobody moved, nobody spoke. All three stared, spellbound, paralysed by rising fear.

Shane watched it step clear of the tide. With sure, strong movements, it loped along the shore, not running, but jogging purposefully like an athlete or a hunter. The weight of its arms, which seemed just a shade too long for the body, made the creature stoop slightly, its bare feet leaving deep imprints in the sand. Running away was out of the question; it was already coming to a halt two metres from where Shane stood.

From under the bony, bulbous eyebrow that protruded from the creature's forehead, the massive eye glared downwards at Shane. Thick lips drew back to expose raw gums and irregular teeth; its upper fangs were noticeably elongated and sharp. With one hand, it scratched the mat of hair covering its chest, then stretched to full height.

"Be not afraid you, you and you," came the low growl.

Wiping wet strands of hair from its face, it manoeuvred a sheathed dagger from the front to the rear of its loincloth, as if to keep it from view.

"Polyphemog the Cyclops make sure nobody else in sight. He see that you are urchins; alone. Others would be problem. I do important job here; harmless ones like you are no risk. After Polyphemog do eye magic, you will not remember. Be not afraid, I no danger."

Shane could hear his heart pounding as he tried to make sense of what he was seeing and hearing. A Cyclops! *Cyclopes?* On Clare Island! *What's standing in front of me is no Greek storybook character; it's real. Flesh and blood. I don't care what it's saying, it wouldn't hesitate to tear me apart with those bare hands.* "We didn't mean to disturb you or anything, sir," he said.

"We were just exploring," said Zara, a catch in her voice.

"I watching you long time," said Polyphemog, breathing loudly through the nose. "Cyclopes see all things very far." Something like a laugh rattled in its throat and crinkles appeared around its eyebrow but quickly vanished.

"My eye will make you forget. Only by that can the presence of Fomorians be a secret."

Shane remained transfixed. Polyphemog reminded him of a heavyweight wrestler but the wild and unkempt appearance didn't suggest gym training was responsible for its build. The guttural accent and strange speech also suggested English wasn't its native tongue.

The Cyclops looked up and down the deserted shoreline. "Look deep into my eye and sleep time come fast. As before I say, be not afraid, Polyphemog use eye magic many times."

His rough-skinned, talon-like hands gently clasped Zara and Tubs by their arms and aligned them closer to Shane. "This secret must always be secret."

Tubs' reply came tumbling out. "I swear we won't tell anyone about meetin' you, mister, honest."

"What if we're not able to forget everything?" whispered Zara.

"Nobody not forget." Polyphemog rested for a few seconds before continuing in a softer monotone. "You look deep; only think sleep, sleep, sleep."

Shane realised that speaking for any length of time seemed to require an extra effort of concentration by Polyphemog. Fighting horror and nausea, he stared mutely into the unblinking eye as it widened, narrowed, refocused and rotated around its large orbit, as if possessed by a life force of its own.

"Eye magic powerful; make you feel slumber then return to your home places. Heavy sleep now; you will remember nothing – nothing – nothing." His voice dropped lower, becoming a persuasive purr.

Shane shot a glance at Tubs and Zara; their mouths were hanging slightly open; they seemed unconcerned, almost relaxed.

Zara spoke with slow deliberation. "What I saw was a dream. I remember nothing."

"I remember nothin'," intoned Tubs.

I can't believe it – it's like that hypnotist in that YouTube vid. But why hasn't it worked on me?

Polyphemog grunted. "It is well. All go now."

Without a moment's hesitation, Tubs and Zara turned, and began dreamily retracing their steps towards the pathway. Shane caught both their shoulders as they passed.

"Wait a sec," he cried but they walked past without breaking stride or acknowledging his presence.

"You," snarled Polyphemog, his left hand around Shane's throat, almost lifting him off the ground. "Why eye magic not make you sleep? It always work." He released his grip.

Coughing, Shane regained his balance, clearing his throat but aware of Polyphemog's animal smell and irregular breathing. *Should I try foot-sweeping the thing's legs and hammering after Tubs and Zara? No... it would take a forklift truck to shift it...*

"This very bad," interrupted Polyphemog, wringing his hands. "Eye magic always good."

"Give it another go, sir," said Shane, massaging his neck.

Polyphemog whipped the dagger free then drew his fingers across his throat. "You forget or death."

Unable to think with the thundering in his ears, Shane gulped. "I'll do my best, really."

"This is last time. Look deep. Now sleep, sleep…"

Mindful of the simmering violence underlining Polyphemog's every action, Shane was determined to concentrate fully on the baleful eye. For what seemed an age, he ordered himself to drop off. *What if I pretend to be hypnotised? No, he'd probably knife me on the spot if he even suspected I was faking…*

"Have you forget?"

Shane took a backward step, aware of the muscle twitching erratically on the Cyclops' temple. "It's just not working today, Mr Polyphemog. Maybe you caught a chill or something?"

He saw the Cyclops' knuckles whiten around the knife as an explosive mix of disappointment and rage clouded the face. "One-eye magic never fails."

As things stand my life isn't worth a sneeze – should I risk knocking the knife away then take my chances? No, this thing doesn't need a weapon – he'd kill a polar bear with those fists. My only hope is to run for it…

"I'm afraid I have to go, Mr Polyphemog."

"You go no places. High Druid always say eye magic is first and last defence. This is problem."

"I'm here, Dad," hollered Shane, waving and fixing his attention on something behind Polyphemog.

As the Cyclops turned, Shane arrowed past, ignoring the howl of rage. As he bolted for the footpath, he felt a huge hand grasp the back of his shirt, jerking him backwards. He was lifted clear of the ground as if he weighed no more than a toy. Enveloped by muscular arms possessing great strength, he felt a sack being roughly wrenched over his hair, then his face. The coarse fabric was soaked with something wet that gave off a pungent odour that made his knees immediately buckle. The last words he heard were, "Eye magic no make him sleep. Big problem…"

As Shane's hold on the conscious world slipped away, the not unpleasant smell reminded him of something vaguely medicinal he had experienced, somewhere in childhood; somewhere back, way back somewhere…

Chapter 5

Mr Donnegan looked up from cleaning *Faith's* windscreen at the two fishermen sitting on the nearby harbour wall. Lean and hard as rifles, they were mending nets, their sweaters beaded with droplets of drizzle.

"Excuse me, lads," he called, "I'm not too sure of the waters around here. Reckon there'll be enough tide to take me back over the Rosmoney sandbanks at this hour?"

The older man removed the cigarette from his mouth and gazed at the distant mainland. "I wouldn't chance it, me; best wait for the tide to turn."

Mr Donnegan's face said it all – getting into Granddad's mooring at low water was now out of the question. He'd have to make the return journey in darkness or else stay overnight on the island; neither option appealed to him. In the distance he saw Tubs and Zara approaching.

"What time do you call this?" He looked over their shoulders then scanned the pier and roadway. "Where's Shane?" he demanded.

"Who?" said Zara, blinking.

"Stop acting the maggot." He squinted again into the distance. "That son of mine really does need a good boot in the tail. Where did you leave him? Have you two been asleep or something."

"I'm thinkin', Mr D. Ah, yes, we left him back there, near the, er, beach."

Mr Donnegan's knuckles tightened on the gunwale. "Finbar, this here's an island. Surrounded by beaches. Where is he, for Pete's sake?"

"Sorry, I just don't know this place that well..."

"A, er, little up the road," Zara said vaguely.

Mr Donnegan vaulted out of the boat on to the jetty. "Bloody daydreamers. Show me where you left him, or we'll never get away from this place."

***

The Garda Sergeant unbuttoned his uniform. "Now let's go back to the beginning, again," he articulated slowly. "This is where the pair of ye say ye left the Donnegan lad, right? On the beach?"

"Er, yes, Sergeant Canny," Zara said, aware she was the centre of a large circle of solemn people. Handpicked by the burly policeman, they were the fittest of the hotel patrons who'd volunteered to search for Shane.

"What time was that?"

"Er, around quarter past five; half five-ish." Zara turned to Tubs for confirmation.

"Um, yes, it was turnin' half five, I think."

The sergeant's brow creased. "Ye two couldn't give a straight answer to save yer blessed lives. Anyways, ye weren't up to any devilment, that much we've established. Ye left together; why didn't ye come back together?"

"Yes, I mean no, sergeant. Shane told me and Tubs, er, to go on ahead and he'd catch up, like."

"Yes, yes, yes," said Tubs, his eyelids flickering. "Shane said he'd catch up, I think…"

"YE THINK?!" exploded the policeman. "We've been scouring this island for three hours; there's neither sight nor sound of the young fella and you tell me think!" He shook his head. "God grant me patience."

"I'm really sorry," whispered Zara, "everything's so fuzzy…"

The hotel owner, Harry Hughes, tutted sympathetically and placed his arm around Zara, to her annoyance. "Most likely shock, sergeant. Maybe something nasty's happened to them; it can affect the memory, you know. Blots things out, like, especially with the younger generation."

Canny switched his attention to gaunt-faced Mr Donnegan. "Fraid I'll have to call out the lifeboat from Achill Island, sir, and the helicopter service. That Tubs fella might knock off a bit of weight by helping us with the night search. I said it before and I'll say it again; them seas may look innocent enough in good weather but many's the rogue wave I've seen do awful things. Awful."

He didn't elaborate, but turned away, jabbing numbers on his mobile.

Zara was crying. The other searchers, many looking tired, self-consciously turned their eyes away, deliberately busying themselves looking at their maps and rummaging in backpacks.

"Nobody's blaming you, Zara," said Mr Donnegan. "It's all down to me."

"But how could *you* be to blame?" she demanded, wiping away her tears. "You weren't even *there*."

"I didn't have to be there, Zara," he said, returning her stare. "The first clue was you and Tubs behaving as if you were hypnotised or something. My boy hasn't been taken by the sea; it's calm out there and isn't he a good swimmer? Something very strange has happened; I'm trying to remember…"

He shook his head as if vainly trying to block a pain erupting from a troubled brain. "Why did I come back to this infernal Island?"

Chapter 6

Shane groggily came to. Covered with a rough blanket and sprawled on a slab of flat rock, he looked around the small, bleak cave. The floor was composed of limestone, worn smooth over centuries. Propping himself on an elbow and suspecting he was dreaming but awake at the same time, he rubbed his eyes. The only exit from the oppressive grotto was barred by a door composed of vertical wooden struts, each the thickness of a man's fist.

Where am I?

He shook his head to clear his brain, staggered upright and tried to push open the heavy door. No chance. *Some sort of natural cavern, with very unnatural bars...*

With his alarm quickly turning to fear, he scanned the rest of the chamber.

In one shadowy corner, a trough had been cut to form a basin on which a stopper and a crude bar of soap lay. A coarse towel hung across the pipe that fed the basin with a constant dribble of water. Three metres above, a strip of fluorescent lighting in the roof threw a mottled whiteness over everything. No windows. The hole in the furthest corner was a toilet of sorts.

I'm a prisoner in some sort of jail. At least it's warm.

His cell lay at the end of a small passage which opened into a wide sprawling vault, encased on all sides by rock. Its openness was sealed in by a further, more distant dome that enveloped the whole area. Much of the vastness was illuminated by the same type of dim lighting, winding up the walls and running across the canopies of irregular stone.

Could all this be another of my nightmares? Who brought me here? Polyphemog? He must have drugged me or something...

One thing seemed certain – there was no escape.

He moved closer to the bars and peeked next door. A similar hovel; same setup; tap, soap, running water.

I hate dripping pipes, especially at night. Always keep me awake, though that's the least of my worries now.

The mesh of cobwebs caught his attention. *Spiders – my only cellmates. I'm starting to talk to myself – first sign of madness? Where would I go even if I could get past that door?*

The sound of approaching feet interrupted his spinning thoughts.

A one-eyed man of powerful build, wearing a kilt and a sleeveless leather tunic, stopped in front of the cell. In one hand he carried a tray, a ring of keys in the other.

"Polyphemog," Shane said, feeling a vague relief. Someone he recognised, at least.

The Cyclops placed the rounded flat slate on the ground, and pulling a wooden baton from his belt, swept it viciously across the bars, barely in time for Shane to whip his fingers away.

"You no speak," he said, his eyebrow prominent and threatening.

Shane backed away, nodding dumbly.

"Me no Polyphemog," the creature growled, jabbing his hairy chest with a thumb. "Me, Agamemnon, jail man."

With his foot, he slid the plate into the cell through the narrow space between door and floor. Gesturing Shane forwards, he pushed a tin mug through the bars.

Ever watchful of the weapon dangling from the jailer's wrist, Shane said, "Thanks, Agamemnon."

Seeing the creature's grip tighten around the truncheon, Shane guessed that Polyphemog might have warned the jailer to expect trickery from his new ward.

The glaring eye scanned for a suggestion of disrespect and seeing none, Agamemnon shuffled out of sight.

These people are far from friendly.

Frightened and numb, he sat on the bed and began gulping down food.

I must've been out for the count for some time; can't remember a thing after the beach. And the grub's nice – fish and some weird sort of rice – tastes like unsweetened tea with a tang of seaweed.

The plate was made of silver. He inspected the chipped mug and crude spoon; they weren't silver, he'd seen better gear chucked in the school's rubbish bins.

Who are these aggressive, brutal people? Cyclopes? Fomorians? But this is the 21st century...

Marching feet. Approaching.

Pushing the food aside, he focused on the passageway.

A long line of men and women were silently filing to a standstill outside the cell, all staring intently at him. Shane relaxed somewhat when he saw the watchers had two eyes; ordinary folk like himself. *Ordinary?* Not quite. All were dressed in colourful, loose-fitting smocks that reached shin and elbow; both sexes similarly clothed in short-sleeved jackets and kilts or skirts, reminding him of extras he'd seen in some old movie somewhere. Excited children were clambering on their fathers' backs to get a better view. Glowering in the background was Agamemnon. Or was it Polyphemog? Scattered about, singly and in groups, stood more of the same one-eyed beings, many wearing leather aprons with tool belts; others held picks and sledgehammers in their rough-skinned hands. Nobody spoke. Shane couldn't decide who was more dumbfounded, the watchers or the watched.

One thing's for sure, these people hate me for some reason.

From the rear a voice shouted, "Execute the invader."
A ripple of approval followed.

The crowd parted as three men pushed through. Two were draped in white togas while the third, striding authoritatively ahead, was smaller and swarthy, wearing a black habit that reached below the ankles and swished as he moved. The loose-fitting cowl partially shadowed his jutting chin and sharp, pointed nose. Seeing Shane for the first time, his thin lips compressed into a straight line. The carved sceptre in his hand completed a demeanour of ruthless authority. Shane shivered. Here was somebody with whom he had never exchanged a word, yet he instinctively knew this man would never lift a finger to help him.

The man rapped the bars with his sceptre before addressing the crowd. "Who is responsible for this?" he said with chilling softness.

As a Cyclops stepped forwards, Shane noticed the crowd was still swelling, overflowing the thoroughfare.

"It me, Indech, me that take him prisoner," Polyphemog said, shuffling from one foot to another. "I see them on Pylos' beach."

"Imbecile. You can see and smell an Up-Worlder for leagues. Why did you not use your eye magic?"

"Please, Indech, three urchins come. I was almost drowned by storm but I not see anybody else. Two invaders I use eye magic on and send them away." He pointed a hairy finger at Shane. "Him – it no work. I try and I try."

"Why didn't you use your mirror, you fool?"

"The boy he try to run so...."

"...Excuses! Must I always be the one to clean up everyone else's mistakes? These other Up-Worlders you encountered – did you allow the full thirty seconds?"

"I think…"

"Leave! I shall decide on your punishment later." Indech turned to address Shane and barked, "Name?"

"I'm Shane Donn…," he began, swallowing hard.

Indech cut him short. "…Shane Dunne is hereby charged with violating Fomorian territory," he said quietly. "Polyphemog did indeed perform eye magic on the other invaders but this enemy has illegally crossed our borders. The law is clear."

His voice dropped further as he paused theatrically, letting the words sink in. "I, Indech, Chief Druid and Defender of the Realm, do find this invader guilty. He will be executed at dawn. Return to your labours."

Shane fought against the sudden incredulity and terror that was sweeping through his body. He stepped forward, pressed his face against the bars, grimly holding them with both hands.

"Sorry to butt in, sir," he said, hoping desperately that he was using a respectful tone, "but I've done nothing wrong."

"Prisoners do not speak unless requested to," murmured Indech with a cold smile.

A new voice, calm and deep, interjected. "A moment, Indech, by your leave."

Shane stared at the tallest of all the two-eyed spectators who raised a hand, a mildly mocking expression on his long, narrow face. Thin as a javelin, his high forehead was bare while his slight stoop marked him as much older than Indech. The deep lines etched into his face gave him a prim, almost scholarly appearance, reminding Shane of grey-haired judges he'd seen on TV. His soft voice carried a sharp, dignified authority yet he addressed Indech as if addressing an unreasonable child at a birthday party.

"This is preposterous, Indech. Ignorance of our laws on the part of the boy, yes; insolence, no. And a death sentence? Unnecessarily harsh, even by your standards."

"Your predictable objection, Connaing, has been noted," said Indech, his tone almost kindly. "Should I wish to know the difference between a Fomorian jig and reel then, and only then, will I consult you. Defence of the realm is my responsibility, not yours."

Unfazed, Connaing continued. "I'm perfectly happy with our laws; your application of them is devoid of the warm milk of mercy."

"Praise from the Minister of Dancing is praise indeed. I have no interest in your music and poetry; only in enforcing the rules that protect our very existence."

"Your sentence is unlawful; the death sentence applies only to adults. The accused is obviously not an adult. Or had you not noticed?"

Another toga-clad man stepped in. "As Court Recorder, I request the prisoner's age be made known."

Connaing bowed then addressed Shane. "What is your age, boy?" he said, emphasising the word boy.

"Fourteen, sir," said Shane, recognising that beneath Connaing's somewhat forbidding exterior, his eyes were kind.

"Indech, I accept full responsibility for Shane Dunne until the king provides us with his judgment. Until then this matter falls outside your domain."

The Recorder nodded. "Connaing is correct. King Tethra has the final say in all death sentence cases."

"But our king still lies in his sick bed…" began Indech.

"…And we all pray," interrupted Connaing smoothly, "that his health be promptly restored. In the meantime…"

Rising on tiptoe, Indech smiled, pressing his face close to Connaing's. "Take the intruder with you," he said cheerfully, "for now, Master of the Dance."

Shane watched the crowd drift away, although some children lingered, staring into his cell. Many were blue eyed and blonde, others had darker complexions; some carried glass bowls containing small fish.

Connaing signalled Agamemnon to pull back the bolt then held the door open. "Come with me, boy."

Shane needed no second invitation.

Chapter 7

With Shane close behind, Connaing pushed through the crowded jail enclosure and ascended the short flight of steps into the great domed enclosure above the cells.

"My home means a walk across the town," said Connaing. With a wry smile he added the word, *boy*. "Do not speak to anyone."

People stopped talking as they approached; some scowled, others shouted insults. Shane tried to remain ramrod straight as he walked, ignoring the splotches of spittle landing on his clothes, focusing only on the skull-grey rock that dominated everything. Above his head the high canopy of rugged limestone was rough and untouched. At ground level, all irregularities had been smoothed down to form footpaths or sculpted into green rectangles, where small trees and plants grew. In the distance, he saw lines of sweating Cyclopes, naked to the waist and supported on a series of wooden scaffolds and platforms, hammering and pounding. They were constructing a wide, downward-leading staircase, so deep even the roof lights and wall torches failed to illuminate the bottom.

Shane remembered Brisbane as a hive of activity but compared with the surrounding tumult of building and engineering, his home city was, well, a morgue. "Mind if I ask a question, sir?" *I've a million. Where do I start?*

"You may address me as Connaing."

"Why do you live, er, underground, Connaing?"

"Thousands of years ago, we were virtually annihilated by our enemies; today our existence relies on our laws and total concealment. Only one person from the Up-World has ever set foot here; you are the second." *His wrinkled face reminds me of old Dr Patton back in Brisbane, who always tried to keep bad medical news from his patients.*

Shane took a deep breath and flung out the question burning his tongue. "Do you think the King will overturn my death sentence?"

"We cannot predict the future but we can seek to influence its course. Your youth has temporarily spared you."

"Fair enough but..." He waved his arm in a circle. "Where exactly am I?"

"Some distance below the surface of Clare Island."

"But islands are made of rock; this place looks hollow, yeah?"

"This was once an active volcano but the lava retracted leaving the interior void and empty."

"How deep do all these caves go?"

"Great distances; nobody knows their true extent; many are unexplored. As one descends towards the volcanic layer, the temperature rises; therefore our climate is never too hot, never too cold."

Connaing pointed to the roofless row of single-storey houses, all with open windows. Shallow ducts supplied each abode with water from culverts that ran through the centre of the narrow road.

"Boiling water is supplied by our geysers, freshwater from above. Our waste liquids drain into the sea while smoke is absorbed by moist layers of compacted soil. Simple but effective systems." He smiled proudly. "My own designs."

"But – these Cyclopes doing all that digging...?"

"...We, the fair-skinned with two eyes, lived on the island of Thera; the Cyclopes lived nearby. After our islands were destroyed by earthquakes, we sailed together to Ireland. Since then, the Cyclopes do the labouring while we are responsible for engineering, teaching, medicine and so on. All that remains of our once great race now resides here."

A short silence fell.

"But, why underground?"

"The Tuatha de Dannan put us to the sword and obliterated us from history. All that remains of our people is right here." He rubbed his furrowed forehead. "Today nobody has even heard of the Fomorians."

"Yes, they have!" Shane said. "My teacher, Mr Stubbs, said the Fomorians were ugly monsters and pirates who... er..."

Oh, me and my big mouth! I've gone and put my foot in it by rubbishing these people and...

"...History is written by the victors, Shane," Connaing interjected softly. "The writings of the Christian monks falsified what really happened; only we know the true version of events. Come."

Shane accompanied Connaing down a short flight of stairs and took a deep breath as it opened into another square, bigger than St. Columbanus' football pitch. A fountain stood in the centre, its four spouts cascading over a life-sized statue of a man that suggested great wisdom and power. A thick volume in one hand, an eagle on his shoulder, the marble sculpture carried the inscription:

Eochu – Magician, Sage, Leader.

Connaing pointed. "That man wrote most of our books, guided us, gave us our Mission, our pride and, perhaps, our future..."

Shane stared down at his trainers, hoping that Connaing mightn't sense his inner confusion. *Do I recognise Eochu from somewhere? Best stay schtum.* The ringing calls from the nearby street vendors cut through his thoughts as did the clack of wooden machinery and the snarling of saws from the passageways close by.

A man shouted, "Come over here, Up-Worlder, and you won't need a trial." An explosion of guffaws followed.

Shane quickly moved away, feeling as if he was walking on a carpet of air through the pages of some history book, confused but amazed. And very afraid.

His jaw sagged on seeing the line of three-storey buildings, hewn from the perpendicular cave walls and fronted by colonnades of varying heights. All had glassless windows or shutters while the entrances were fronted by drapes or centrally-parted curtains, rather than doors. Inside, orbs hung from the ceilings, throwing off wan illumination, weaker than the strips of lighting that lined each narrow thoroughfare.

These people are far more advanced than I first thought… "Are those, er, electric lights, Connaing?"

Connaing nodded. "We produce hydroelectricity from our underground rivers. The remainder is supplied by the eels we breed and from deep-sea cucumbers – species extinct in the Up-World. The cucumbers we cultivate as floating batteries store solar energy during the day and release it by night. The Cyclopes take them to the surface when the tide is right and retrieve them when fully charged. You happened upon Polyphemog with a battery-crate torn free by the storm. He's an excellent gardener, you know."

Gardener? Gladiator more like.

The smell of hot metal and wood hit Shane's nostrils. The adjacent alleyway was a warren of stalls and shed-like structures where men worked, surrounded by timber and planks of wood. Further on, two perspiring smithies stood over a forge, one toiling over a bellows while the other hammered red-hot lengths of iron. At the far end he could see a line of aproned workers astride revolving wheels, toiling with moulds of rotating wet clay.

"Each family has its own workplace or cubicle. Today is our market day, when we barter and this evening we will sing, enjoy ourselves and tell our stories."

How can they build a whole underground town with nothing more than muscle and brain-power? "This is, well, something else, Connaing."

Acknowledging the compliment, Connaing smiled. "Our skills are handed down from generation to generation. Our medicine men treat most ailments whilst loyalty overrides all other concerns. We have four housing sections – for manual workers, then engineers, the third for the healers and teachers; the fourth for the King and his family."

The King! A shiver shook Shane as he remembered his upcoming court appearance. "Your King – he's a, er, fair-minded guy, is he? Does he always listen to Indech?"

"Indech is the King's advisor and regards me as his sworn enemy."

A group of four young men, armed with short staves appeared into the open from the shadows. Approaching Connaing, the stumpy, muscular leader said, "We're here to take care of the Up-Worlder, we don't need the king's approval." He turned to the others. "Do we?"

All nodded assent and shuffled forward.

"You're never far from trouble, are you Uscar?" said Connaing, his tone friendly. "Let us pass."

As Shane watched Uscar's knuckles tighten around his staff, Connaing drew back his toga exposing the short sword dangling from his belt. He grasped the handle. Still sounding amicable, he said, "Isn't it time for bed, boys?" striding past the glowering four without a backward glance. "Keep up, Shane," he added cheerfully, "we're nearly there."

"Who were they, Connaing?"

"Members of Indech's Youth Movement. These are troubled times."

From the clutter of nearby dwellings came the sounds of cooking and cleaning, superimposed on voices calling, talking and arguing. The aroma of frying fish made Shane salivate. From nowhere he remembered his football jersey hanging on the back of his bedroom door; the smell of his father's lumpy potato cakes and... *This wishful thinking's getting me nowhere. How do I escape?*

From an upper room came the rich notes of a harp, accompanied by a girl singing. Her voice made Shane's skin prickle as the song carried and reverberated along the narrow passageway, as if amplified by some powerful PA system. It reminded him of opera music he'd once heard in a Brisbane shopping mall – the words had made no sense but just like the Fomorian song, the emotion in the woman's voice had affected him in a way he couldn't quite understand.

Connaing pulled aside the frontal drape. "Welcome to my home."

Chapter 8

Shane immediately smelt the airy freshness. The house was spotless. The walls were adorned with tapestries depicting ocean and domestic scenes of Ancient Greece. Illuminated by a multi-coloured orb of frosted glass hanging from the ceiling, the centre of the room was dominated by a bust of Eochu on a plinth, the same eagle on his shoulder. Two steps led to a kitchen where simmering pots hung above an open fire. Further to the rear, drying clothes were suspended by pairs of mussel shells on vines of string-like seaweed.

"Fortune to all who cross our threshold," a voice called and a tall woman entered. Pushing back blonde wisps of greying hair, her attention was riveted on Shane. "Is this the boy? So young to be tried for…."

"…No such talk, my dear," said Connaing with exaggerated brightness. "Ceithlinn, this is Shane."

As he moved awkwardly forwards, Shane became even more embarrassed, realising that the Fomorian mode of introduction was very different to what he was used to. Instead of palms being grasped and held, each participant held the other below the elbow, making the greeting an arm clasp, rather than a handshake.

Behind Ceithlinn, he saw a young man and girl enter the room. Both were stunningly handsome with blonde hair and green eyes. Their high cheekbones and chiselled features had the veneer of polished porcelain. Each wore armlets under their tunics, the girl a twisted collar of gold around her neck. Most striking to Shane was their similarity, and although the boy was clearly older, their faces were virtual mirror images of each other. Hands clasped in front, they stood erect. At ease but watchful.

"My children," said Connaing. "Elatha is fourteen, Lugh seventeen. Meet Shane Dunne."

Lugh, bowed and unsmilingly shook hands, Fomorian style. As if to get the business over quickly, he clicked his heels together and smartly retreated, allowing his sister to take his place.

"Elatha, you must have been the one, er, playing, I mean singing…" mumbled Shane, finding the words difficult.

The girl's serious demeanour softened and turned into a smile, showing perfect rows of milk-white teeth. As Shane would never forget, the room seemed to light up with the warmth that radiated outwards, filling him with strange sensations he'd never felt before.

"You liked it?" she said, turning a curve of golden lock behind an ear, exposing a green earring.

"The harp's my favourite instrument," he said without hesitation, promising himself that if he ever got out alive, he would learn how to play the harp, no matter what.

Aware of the dryness in his mouth, he saw that Elatha's loveliness wasn't like the girls on TV. Her beauty was something in a real person kind of way, as if there were sincere feelings behind that sculpted face.

"My instrument is called the Harp of Fourfold Music, once played by our bards of old."

"Oh, I see," he said, looking down at his hands. *Say something; something sensible; anything…* "I'd have loved to hear those old guys play," he added quickly, the words sounding calmer than his turbulent emotions. "I bet they were fantastic! Not as good as you, though."

What's up with me? Why do I want her to like me?

Ceithlinn interrupted the exchange by appearing from the kitchen with a tray of steaming bowls. "Everyone please to the table."

Sitting down, Shane straightened his empty plate and fiddled with the cutlery, struggling to find something worthwhile to say. *What do you say to people who feed you yet might cart you off to be executed the next day?*

"This is our speckled rice," Ceithlinn interrupted brightly, serving a stew of sorts accompanied by a chunky loaf of bread.

"How can you grow stuff down here?" Shane said, itching to impress Elatha as much as anything else.

"The retreating lava left plenty of mineral-rich clay and ash behind," said Connaing. "Mixed with various seaweeds, we get very good yields."

Ceithlinn passed around a large bowl filled with crisp, multi-coloured seaweed. Shane took a mouthful and in spite of his misgivings, found it delicious. The sharp peppery leaves mingled with soft ones that oozed a creamy sap, while others dangled tiny berries that reminded him of juicy mushrooms.

"These plates aren't like the silver ones in the, er, jail," he ventured eventually.

"We salvaged those from two galleons of the Spanish Armada," said Connaing.

"I bet all that silver and stuff is worth a packet?"

Connaing frowned. "Packet?"

"A lot of money."

"We're only interested in what is useful – the silver bowls make excellent receptacles for collecting water." He leant back in his chair. "In 1943 a German submarine sank off the lighthouse. We salvaged much oil."

"I don't remember reading about that," said Shane, determined to sound mature and well read. *Best not let them know that the only things I know about WW II come from the TV and films...*

"Also, a container ship that perished with all hands provided us with the most valuable haul – lights that allow us to cultivate certain foodstuffs without using soil – hydroponics."

"Hydro ponicks?"

"Lamps that produce artificial sunlight so we grow the fresh fruit that keeps our skin healthy. I'm Advisor in Applied Engineering but Indech won't permit us to use Up-World technology that he considers threatening to our way of life."

Shane swallowed hard, trying to imagine what life would be like without his mobile, iPad, computer...

"...We are allowed certain utilities from the Up-World; things *we actually need.* Indech and his Council of Culture make all such decisions although their real concern is keeping power."

"Forget all that," said Elatha, smiling. She cupped her chin in her hands and swivelled to regard Shane. "Tell me about the real Up-World. All we know is what Indech and the Watchers tell us..."

"...I know enough about your Up-World," growled Lugh, regarding Shane through half-closed eyes. "Given half a chance you people would invade and overrun us. In the past, more Fomorians were killed than there are stars in the sky or drops of dew upon the meadows in springtime."

"Hold on a sec," said Shane. "That had nothing to do with me, I mean, us."

"Up-Worlders are all the same," Lugh shot back. "Never to be trusted."

"We're all entitled to our individual views," said Connaing, holding up his hand for peace. "Our great defeat took place so long, long ago."

"You neglect something else, father."

"What?"

"After we were overwhelmed by the Tuatha De Dannan, our heroes were buried standing upright, fully armed. On that hill above the battlefield they still face the enemy, awaiting the moment of resurrection, ready to again protect the Fomorians. Those men knew then, as I do now, that the heartless Tuatha de Dannan nor the Up-World, will ever change."

"Please," said Elatha, drumming the table with her fingers, "no more talk of death or battles. Shay-An, tell me about those things that are called discos? And malls of shops?"

Seeing Lugh's fists clench, Shane decided to change the subject. "Could I use the gents, please?"

"Gents?" grunted Lugh.

"You know, the, er, toilet, like…"

"All our toilets," said Connaing proudly, "flow down into a chute leading to the volcano. My own design based on…"

"…Please, Father!" said Elatha.

"We call it the release closet," interrupted Ceithlinn softly. "It's outside the rear door. I'll prepare your bed."

Shane regarded her gratefully, noticing for the first time how calm and kindly she appeared. *You'd be glad to see a face like that if you were worried or sick… Was Mum like her? I wish I could remember…*

Ignoring his lined reflection in the toilet mirror, he tried to dismiss his troubled thoughts and longings. In the murky outside light, he studied the peaceful family scene through the crack in the curtains.

How many weird things and coincidences has it taken to drag me into this place? And how come these people are up to speed on what's happening in the real world?

He stepped into the crude WC and drew the drape across the entrance.

I must escape.

Chapter 9

Shane awoke with Ceithlinn staring down at him, a layer of folded clothes draped across her arm. Plagued by disturbing dreams filled with anxiety and sweetness in equal measure, he struggled to get his bearings. Part of him wanted to snuggle deeper into the blankets and go back to sleep – anything to keep his mind off...

"Try these on," Ceithlinn said, "Breakfast is ready. The king is still unwell so he will not be able to hear your case. Are these not good tidings?"

She left without waiting for an answer. Shane tried to decide which was better – to have his case heard sooner, or later?

In military kit, Lugh was already at the table, broodily chewing a stick of celery. As Shane arrived, Elatha surveyed his kilt, long stockings and a tunic that was two sizes too large.

"Charming," she said, giggling into the palm of her hand.

Ceithlinn entered as Shane was finishing a breakfast that initially reminded him of roadkill in mushy sauce but actually tasted great.

"Elatha plans to show you around this afternoon," she said. "Perhaps you might have an interest in accompanying Lugh to the early army training session?"

Wait. Didn't Connaing say the Fomorians weren't into war stuff any longer? Who are they afraid of? I've got to learn more.

He looked enquiringly across at Lugh who responded by saying, "Every male does military training four days a week."

"Why's that?"

"Indech wishes our young men to become warriors – a strong body can develop an even tougher mind, he says. There will no longer be any couch potatoes here."

Couch potato? How come this guy speaks modern stuff when half the time they seem to speak Shakespeare? They have no TV or...

"Would you care to join in, Up-Worlder? Indech has given me permission to take you, should you so wish..."

Shane continued chewing. "Well, I guess... I don't know, it's not really my thing..." *I mustn't let this guy rile me...*

"Maybe you are scared, Up-Worlder?"

As the challenge hung in the air, Ceithlinn said, "That's enough, Lugh. Far too many young men get injured fighting and boxing with the Cyclopes. You should not goad your father's guest."

Lugh raised his hands in surrender. "I only want our *guest* to feel at home, mother," he said.

Shane made up his mind. "It's no bother, Ceithlinn. I'm all for giving it a whack."

Lugh raised his eyebrows. "You surprise me. Well, maybe you'll benefit from the experience. But don't blame me if you get hurt."

Shane stood up. "I'm ready when you are."

Lugh was already exiting the storeroom, carrying a pair of wooden swords and oval shields. He threw two long staves to Shane, then jerked his head towards the door. "You're unlikely to get a warm welcome from the others. Do not worry, I will look after you."

"Well... thanks, Lugh."

Although he knew it was morning, Shane felt the absence of sunshine and clouds unsettling. After descending three flights of stairs, they came to the end of a low tunnel which opened into a flat spacious arena. Numerous youths stood around, some in small groups, most in pairs. All wore protective pads on their arms and legs. Long ropes dangled from above and a series of wooden hurdles lined the surrounding track. In the foreground, two gloved boxers were sparring, enclosed by a ring of scraggy ropes constructed from sea vines. He was surprised he could translate the sign in Ancient Greek which read: "TRAINING AREA."

"Excuse me, Lugh," said Shane, "everybody speaks English, so why's everything in Greek?"

"After leaving Thera to come here, we spoke Greek but slowly switched to Fomorian or Gaelic. Today we use English but we can speak all three fluently. As soon as they can talk, children can speak Greek and Irish."

"Three languages?"

"Father claims it is another Fomorian mystery, as evolution alone cannot be responsible."

"Aren't you afraid I might try and escape?"

"Impossible," said Lugh, smiling. "The Gates are the only exits. You'd never find them and they're always locked. And guarded. Mind you, there is one other way out."

"Where?"

"All who've tried to get out that way have drowned. Except one."

"Who was that?"

"Many years ago, a hothead made it. But it didn't do him any good. He died for his trouble."

"Oh, right."

Shane regarded his surroundings. *For a military school it's pretty dismal; it looks as if it was built before the Romans arrived or whoever came before them.* From the ceiling, four large circular targets hung, arrows and javelins protruding from the pockmarked wood. In a corner, a cumbersome wooden catapult sat, its wheels covered in cobwebs. *The whole place looks as if it's been copied from the pages of some ancient army manual.*

He watched a Cyclops approach, his head covered with a leather cap with dangling ear tufts. Looking as if he'd got out the wrong side of bed he addressed Lugh but pointed his staff at Shane.

"Why prisoner here?"

"He trains with me this morning."

The Cyclops scowled. "Pads put on. In line. Positions. Spears."

Shane walked past the line of hunched young males staring from behind shields. Made from many layers of hide and rimmed with bronze, the shields were sewn together with leather thongs and bound to wicker frames. Most were round but some were in the shape of the figure eight.

Everyone bunched up in front of the instructor called Polycrates. As the barrel-shaped Cyclops ran through the basics of hand to hand combat with sword and shield, Shane found it difficult to comprehend the Cyclops' accent, never mind the garbled instructions.

"Lugh and prisoner," hollered Polycrates, signalling them to the fore. "First to fight."

No introductory bowing to opponent; no time to prepare or even tighten arm pads – so unlike Shane's karate class in Brisbane. This wasn't Lugh of the breakfast table but a lunging battering ram of bone and sinew. Shane backed away, blocking and parrying as best he could, tears rising unbidden as Lugh's heavy weapon crashed against his shoulders and knuckles. Suddenly tripping then sprawling to the ground, he felt Lugh's wooden blade crunch against his neck.

"Perish," came the triumphant shout, as Lugh raised the weapon aloft.

The Cyclops called, "Up-Worlder lose."

Loud applause marked the end of the one-sided contest. Shane struggled upright, determined not to show any sign of pain or humiliation but that's exactly what he was feeling, bad pain and deep humiliation. He dusted himself down and sucked blood from the back of his hand, aware that Lugh's sneer was growing more pronounced, if that was possible.

It was more of the same at javelin and bow and arrow as win-at-all-costs Lugh fought, cheated and connived his way to victory in every contest. There could be no mistaking the instructor's contempt as he announced the same call after each event, "Up-Worlder lose."

Shane had decided that Fomorian training was not for him. It bore no resemblance to the schoolyard scuffles back in Oz. Nor to the skullduggery on the football pitch behind the ref's back. This was gruelling combat, intended to keep a people in a state of war readiness. Everyone fought with a passion he'd never seen or imagined before.

These guys couldn't care less about getting onto football teams, only with becoming part of some warrior elite.

The final session involved staves in the boxing ring. Dispirited and pretty much black with bruises, Shane felt as if time was standing still. *One final round with this vicious machine then I'm off the hook. Mind you, I'd like just one chance to show what I can do...*

Previously he'd been paying the same level of attention as in Mr Kavanagh's maths class, but this time he made sure he soaked up the Cyclops' every directive before entering the ring.

Mr Kavanagh; school; normality. They belong in another dimension. I never thought it possible for any sane person to wish for a long bout of algebra...

"Fight," hollered the instructor.

Teeth clenched, Shane shouted. "I have a question please, sir."

"He wishes to run to the Up-World," shouted someone.

"He needs the release closet," came another voice.

"Speak," barked the instructor.

"Can I use any part of my body, sir, as well as my weapon?"

"Body is weapon too. Hands to hold. Legs to stay up."

"Legs to run away," came another wisecrack.

"Fight."

Lugh leapt from the corner, twirling his staff like a bandleader showing off his baton skills. In a blur of movement, he cracked Shane's calves then, performing a pirouette, rained further blows in rapid succession. The spectators loved it. Shane slowly got to his feet, conscious of the defensive openings Lugh was leaving to anyone who understood the rudiments of martial arts.

The appreciative yowls increased.

Lugh danced forwards again. Wily leopard that he was, he remained focused on Shane's face – his first mistake. As Shane distracted him with a clumsy sideways movement, Lugh automatically raised his weapon to block the attack that would never come – second mistake. He hadn't seen Shane's footsweep coming before it crashed against his ankle, knocking him off balance. Shane advanced and balancing on one leg, delivered a flying kick to Lugh's temple, sending him sprawling.

"A full Mawashi Geri," Shane panted. "Courtesy of Sensei Tanaka, Brisbane Karate School."

The crowd had never witnessed their champion being downed, nor seen such effective footwork. As Shane swung his staff as if to strike, Lugh raised both arms to protect his head and neck from the inevitable blow but it never came. Shane had thrown the weapon aside. Polycrates grabbed him by the shoulder as he tried to leave the ring.

"Punish enemy. No walk away."

"I don't hit people when they're down, sir."

"Attack very well. Head kick very well." Shane heard the new note of respect in the Cyclops' voice.

"It's called karate, sir."

"Car-at-ty?"

"Japanese self-defence. Would you like me to show you a few basic moves?"

"You no show anything to me. Hand bleed. Attend yonder for strapping."

Shane was leaving the ring when Lugh, his face burning, leapt to his feet and attacked from behind with a brutal rabbit punch. Defeat was hard enough for Lugh to take but the humiliation of being spared, by an outsider at that, was by far the greater insult. As he moved forwards to drive home a second punch, the Cyclops' blow to the solar plexus sent him crashing to the floor.

"You fight right," Polycrates growled, pointing his staff at Lugh. "You bad loser. Retreat to corner or suffer bad."

Seeing Shane being disentangled from between the ropes, Lugh shouted, "Never turn your back on an enemy."

A weak supportive cheer followed from the watching crowd but Shane noticed that this time, some of the onlookers were looking at him, not Lugh, with admiration in their eyes.

Ignoring his throbbing neck, Shane picked himself up and smiled. "Have a nice day, Lugh."

Chapter 10

Connaing was waiting outside the training area, his face even more lined than Shane remembered.

"Where did you learn to fight like that?" he said, breaking into step with Shane.

"I'm sort of OK at karate."

"That was no OK fight, as you describe it. That was a duel in a military centre where, until today, Lugh was undefeated champion." As if making up his mind about something he added, "An idea has struck me; I'd like you to visit our library."

"I'm not great at reading, Connaing, but a seriously old library sounds really…"

"…There's something there I'd like you to see. Ah, there's the librarian. Ruad!"

The distant figure turned, his round shape and bald head reminding Shane of a garden gnome dressed in an oversized toga.

"Would you mind," said Connaing, "showing our, er, visitor, around?"

The librarian didn't reply but caught Connaing by the elbow and marched him some steps away, out of Shane's earshot.

Why don't they want me to hear what they're saying? By feigning an interest in his surroundings, Shane could just about pick up snippets of their conversation.

Connaing's face was flushed as he spoke, half in whispers, "…Friends of mine have gone missing … Homer's Cyclopes are in open rebellion … in the Catacombs..."

Did I hear that right – Catacombs?

The exchange became less audible to Shane as their heads bent closer together. Both men suddenly looked across at Shane. *They're definitely talking about me…*

"…never, Ruad, have I seen a youngster with such skills."

"…no matter. He cannot enter the library. You know the rules."

"You owe me; remember when I…"

"…no need to bring that up. All right then, once; only for you."

As the pair separated, Connaing waved Shane forwards. "Our librarian is eager to show you around," he said, avoiding meeting Shane's gaze. "Ah, here comes my daughter."

Elatha scanned Shane's cuts and bruises. There was no need for her to ask where they'd come from; Shane knew she knew. Before she could speak, Ruad marched away and signalling him to follow, led the way to the end of a deserted corridor and unlocked the heavy library door.

"Aren't you coming in, Elatha?" asked Shane.

"They will not allow me to enter."

"I'm not having that; let me have it out with what's-his-name and…"

"…It is the law."

"Law or no law I'm…"

Her voice dropped. "You are in enough trouble already, Shay-An. You must learn respect."

"Keep your hair on, I'm only trying to help."

Instead of the rows of books Shane had been expecting, the low-ceilinged chamber was lined with widely-spaced tables, on which sat glass cases of varying sizes. Each cabinet contained a single tome; some small and bulky, others over half a metre long. A box of gloves sat on every table. Walking between the rows, he saw that each volume appeared ancient, its author's name printed on the exterior. Aloud he read off the titles: *Thucydides, Pythagoras, Euripides...*

"Hmm, your pronunciation is flawless," said Ruad. "These are original Ancient Greek works from our forefathers, two and a half thousand years ago."

"Really?" said Shane.

"Careful! Can't you read the sign? Parchment is fragile and must be handled with care. That's why I keep the temperature controlled."

"Why the gloves, Ruad?"

"They are made from transparent seaweed, to ensure idiots like you do not soil the pages with grime. I cover the books weekly with a thin layer of powdered fungi that protects them from decay."

"But I thought only the king and the high council were allowed in here?"

"Sometimes exceptions are made," Ruad muttered. "For people like *you*. The Fomorian books are over there."

"But our history teacher, Mr Stubbs, told us the Ancient Irish weren't into writing. He said everything was passed on by word of mouth."

"Your history teacher was ignorant," Ruad snapped. "Our scribes recorded much. Our journeys around the Mediterranean taught us glass making, how to extract dye from seashells; how to forge metal weapons. In the Land-Between-Two-Rivers, before we eventually arrived in Ireland, we watched as words were inscribed on tablets of clay."

"Sounds like some trip," muttered Shane.

Ruad sniffed. "On landing we were welcomed by the Tomb People... astronomers and engineers who constructed temples as part of their earthly Mission. They helped us build our first Fomorian settlement before the Tuatha de Dannan destroyed everything."

"Really?"

Seeing the librarian's set expression, Shane decided to change the subject. "Don't you have any sort of er, normal books, sir?" he said airily.

"There − the Works of Eochu; he was once head sorcerer of the Tuatha de Dannan, masters of the occult."

"Well, they're long dead, eh?" Seeing the librarian's wince, he added, "Aren't they?"

"Just like the Fomorians?" answered Ruad grimly.

As the question hovered, the librarian led Shane across the narrow vestibule carpeted by wickerwork that absorbed their footfalls. He pointed. "This is Eochu's section."

As Shane's attention was taken by the first book, he felt a buzzing in his ears. *Those weird signs on the leather cover look familiar...*

"Can I have a closer look, sir?"

Under the librarian's sharp scrutiny, Shane slid his hands into a pair of gloves before carefully peeling back the book's cover. The first page depicted two hawks staring outwards, their brilliant colours giving them a lifelike vitality.

"Umm, have I seen this... before...?" mumbled Shane, rubbing a hand across his forehead.

The librarian's fingers biting into his arm cut off Shane in midsentence. "You're wasting my time," said Ruad, a new, tighter note in his voice. "Let's get this over; behold the Fomorian Tablet."

Shane glanced at the flat, upright slab, the height of a washing machine. Standing on wooden supports half a metre above the floor, it was covered in dense rows of symbols and characters, all in an alphabet he'd never seen before.

"Does it say anything interesting, sir?"

"These words foretell our future."

"So *this* is what Connaing wanted me to see?"

"Why else would I let an Up-Worlder in here? Imprinted thousands of years ago, these lines foretold our defeat by the Tuatha de Dannan; the death of Eochu, the rise of Indech and..." He paused.

"...And?" prompted Shane.

"... a youth who would save us."

"From what?"

Ruad scowled. "Enough questions. You listen; I'll translate." He bent down and running an index finger beneath the words, began to read aloud.

"...Great will be the New Arrival,
The One of young years,
Who will come without fanfare or trumpet,
Of other blood mixed with ours
To lead the Fomori back to strength.
Speckled salmon will leap from the white womb
Of the dim sea upon which he looks.
From the House of Hades he will grind our enemies.
He a tree with blossom and fruit will be
Heavy with the vine's veritable fragrance;
Unlike his murdered father and mother, he is wood without decay,
On which are leaves of golden hue."

When he'd finished, Ruad looked expectantly at Shane. "Do these things sound familiar to you?"

This is bonkers; no way could this whacko poem have anything to do with me..."It sort of reminds me of the Shakespeare play we're doing at school, it's called..."

"...This is *not* a play," blurted Ruad, making no attempt to hide his exasperation. "Everything that is written here has come to pass."

"Everything?"

"So far, in a manner of speaking."

Shane shrugged his shoulders. "It's nothing to do with me."

The librarian's growl broke the ensuing silence. "This prophecy says..."

"...Look, Ruad, I've no mixed blood. Dad's very much alive and he's as Irish as they come. Mum was also Irish. She wasn't murdered either, see? Whoever the prophecy is about, I'm not involved, got that?"

He saw a light die in Ruad's eyes.

"But... our Tablet has never been wrong. All our predictions..."

"...I'm not saying your slab's got it wrong; I guess your hero will turn up one of these days..."

Ruad had fallen silent, pressing his index finger hard against his teeth. When he eventually spoke, his response was bitter. "Don't waste any more of my time. Go."

Making for the door Shane was at a loss at what to say. "Sorry you sound so disappointed, Ruad; I... will I let myself out?"

The librarian didn't answer. His shoulders sagging, he remained staring at the tablet, an unreadable expression on his face.

Chapter 11

"What part of our tour did you most enjoy, Shay-An?"

Watching a row of Cyclopes working the long tracts of vegetables below, Shane bit his lip. He liked the way she pronounced his name, placing the emphasis on the second syllable, making it two words, not one. Sounded so different, so her. Hesitating, he wished he could bring himself to say that of all the things he'd seen, she was best, by far. But the words refused to sit comfortably on his tongue as the opportunity hovered then passed. *How many important moments in people's lives might have turned out differently if someone had had the guts to say what they were really thinking...*

"I still don't get how the Cyclopes make those crystal things?"

"Don't you ever pay attention? The Cyclopes excel at heavy labour, we make jewellery from sili-crystal."

"Why are they silly?"

"It's you who are silly, Shay-An," she snapped.

Oops! She's getting a bit touchy; I'd better watch it...
"You mean glass?"

"Here we call it sili-crystal, made from silicon." She lightly touched his cheek. "You don't know much about these things, do you, Up-Worlder?"

Not wishing to admit neither chemistry nor history were his strong point, Shane didn't respond.

"Also, our women have always had the same rights as men; free to marry whoever they wish. They even fought together with men in battle..." She hesitated, blushing.

"So?"

"They, um, always fought, naked."

"An army of men and women in their birthday suits; that must've been some sight, yeah?"

They smiled shyly at each other and as they looked away she handed him a small cluster of rounded stones. "For you," she said.

Made of smooth black glass, all perforated in the centre, the stones were suspended on a circular leather thong. A tiny bronze button carrying small hieroglyphics was locked into the centre of each marble. They glowed weakly in his palm.

"Er, great, Elatha, thanks. They'll always remind me of you... What, er, are they?"

"Gems of the Tomb People, thousands of years old."

Shane stared silently at the stones, embarrassed that he had nothing to give her in return.

"Fomorians always bestow the first gift, Shay-An. Your chance will come later."

"Can your One-Eyes swim?"

"Every Fomorian can swim like a dolphin from birth but not the Cyclopes. Our powerful noses smell Up-Worlders at a distance, as do the Cyclopes who also have their eye magic." She pointed to a series of wide pools in the distance, dotted with the swirls of moving fins. "Yonder is where the Cyclopes rear our fish." She frowned. "I wonder why the eye magic did not work on you, Shay-An? Perhaps you are – different from other Up-Worlders?"

He would remember their eyes locking and would later kick himself for not telling her that she was *very different. And special.* As the opportunity hovered fleetingly then evaporated, she held his hand.

"Elatha, that far pool; I don't see any fish moving about..."

She released his hand. "We must get back," she said, her face clouding. "That is the Execution Pool," she added in a small voice.

The sudden fearful silence made Shane shiver. *Will I be floating in that very pool tomorrow...?* "About my trial, Elatha, do you reckon..."

With a sudden, exaggerated cheerfulness, she clapped her hands. "I will race you home," she called, sprinting down the adjacent passageway. Shane didn't move. *I'll never have a better chance to explore on my own. I'll take the opposite route to Elatha...*

Taking two steps at a time he began the descent via the steeper set of stairs towards the lower reaches of the kingdom.

Only naked limestone was visible when he reached the narrow, dimly-lit corridor at the bottom of the flight. The vegetable plots he'd expected were nowhere to be seen. As the stairs became more vertical, his instincts and senses were shouting that something was wrong. *You're lost. Admit it.*

He stopped to get his bearings. First he contemplated turning back but decided to make the most of the opportunity to explore.

The more I know my way about, the better my chances...

It took ten minutes to reach the lowest level. Being lost in such surroundings wasn't a nice feeling – reminding him of the clammy fear of his dreams. Ahead, a distant glow was throwing spider shapes across the low canopy overhead. He felt the acrid tang of sulphur in his throat; *I must be close to those volcanic tunnels that Connaing was on about...*

The clatter overhead made him jump. He watched as a jumble of vegetable peelings and fish heads came cascading from somewhere above, almost in slow motion, then tumbled into the duct that ran close to the stairway. He counted to twenty before he heard an indistinct whoosh from somewhere below. His attention was caught by the nearby flight of stairs leading to an arcade almost obliterated by shadow. Two wooden doors stood on each side of the passageway, a barely legible sign hanging over each entrance: *House of Cerrunos, House of Hades, House of Heroes* and *House of Armour.*

This is a chance to figure things out without someone watching over me.

He hesitated as he approached the *House of Hades.* Suddenly a shiver passed across his heart. *"My sixth sense is telling me that someone has just walked over my grave...!*

Chapter 12

The door was sickeningly familiar. The three interconnecting circles carved into the wood; that same eye and pervading sense of suffocation – no doubt about it – *this is the location of my recurrent nightmare!* He hesitated, fighting back the swell of dread.

Under the row of carved human heads that arched above the entrance, the opening was buttressed by two pillars, each comprising a life-sized demonic figure. Crudely sculpted, both stood with folded arms, two horns protruding from each skull, their hollowed eyes and mouths full of inky emptiness. *I recognise these!* He knew he had to enter, to once and for all confront the horror that had long plagued his nights. Choking back a sob, he pulled back the bolt and pushed against the door.

A long corridor stretched into a widening gloom. He couldn't tell if the light came from the distant volcano or from concealed electrical strips because *he could see in the darkness!* Unable to think clearly, he swallowed hard and plunged on. Numerous alcoves had been funnelled into the walls, each leading into an individually named, small circular room. A grime-covered bronze shield hung outside each chamber. The first three names read: *MORC, TETHRA, OGHAMA.* The dismally bare interiors were ringed with shelves containing rows of small urns. He was in no doubt that here were stored the cremation ashes of past Fomorian chieftains. He'd never felt so alone in all his life.

WHOOSH!

Initially, he assumed the sound was made by some passing bird that had become trapped in the tunnel. *How can anything live at this depth below the ground?* He whipped round. *Nothing there.*

But something had definitely ruffled his hair. In the eerie stillness, a slight movement on the ground caught his attention. Was his imagination playing tricks? No, there could be no doubt. Layers of dust on the floor had begun to gently swirl and drift, as if borne gently upwards on some mysterious wind. Spiralling towards the roof, the coils were condensing into individual shapes, each slowly taking the ghostly form of a human head and shoulders.

Watching numbly, he felt he was hallucinating as the soft murmurings coming from the phantoms' mouths, slowly changed to heart-rending pleadings, as if from people calling across lightyears of space or from barely visible galaxies.

These writhing horrors' arms are stretching out to grasp me. Then they retract. That one was almost at my shoulder before vanishing into nothing. I can still hear its piteous wailing; one moment they have partial human forms; next, their shapes swirl in and out of focus. Some move quickly, others in slow motion; their lips move but I hear nothing until they evaporate. Some are silent but I daren't stare at them; their faces are so contorted by some intolerable distress... Somewhere in the upper air, beyond his field of view, came a woman's keening.

He staggered onwards, each tiny hair on his neck standing on end as invisible fingers pulled at his skin and clothes. He moved through the twisting, nebulous mass, as if passing in and out of clouds of colourless smoke, while the wraiths seemed to warm themselves against his skin. A succession of cold brushing sensations shot through his body while the spirits' repeated pleas made him jam his palms over his ears. A penetrating, insistent voice suddenly resonated above all the others.

"My son. My son. *My son!*"

Cold oil slid through Shane's veins, chilling his blood as he raised his eyes to see a man's face and red-rimmed eyes ravaged by some unbearable tragedy. Shane attempted to run, determined to exit the hateful place, no matter what. The lamentations fell silent as he lost his footing and lay helplessly on his back. A metre overhead, the spirit shimmered.

"Do not run, my son. Time is short."

Trying to keep hold of his sanity and almost incoherent, Shane stuttered, "I am not your, your...your son. My Dad is..."

"...I am your father; at your birth I witnessed the shrivelled toe on your right foot."

Shane stopped breathing. *Who could see, who could possibly know, about my deformed toe?*

The spirit's face burned with a strange hypnotic fervour. *"You are Lorcan, my son."*

Although his head was spinning, Shane felt his terror recede, transforming into a burning and macabre curiosity. He was becoming aware of some bond between himself and this ghost, something, even when he thought about it later, he couldn't explain nor comprehend.

"Please, whatever you are," he croaked, "I'm not Lorcan, I'm Shane. My Dad's Paddy Donnegan. My Mum's dead."

"I am Bres, your father. I was the king's son." His voice became sharper, more impassioned. "What I tell you may freeze your young blood. I was the Head Watcher, your mother was Emelda, the loveliest of all on Clare Island. I eloped with her. You are our son." The spirit stopped to catch its breath. "On returning here, Indech murdered your mother and me."

"Murdered?"

"We were drowned in the pool."

New, conflicting emotions were ripping Shane apart as he tried to stand up. *Could it be remotely possible, that in this pit of doom, this ravaged apparition could really be, my... murdered Dad?*

There was something plausible, horribly believable about every word the ghost spoke. *This is too much for me to take in.*

Bres' voice was weakening. "Indech ripped off my ring - which now braids his hair. You wear my other ring, it summoned me to allow us this short time together."

Shane strained to catch the faltering words. "...Indech will kill... to possess that ring. Lorcan... on reaching manhood, the eldest Fomorian son is honour bound to avenge his father... for this... most foul murder..."

As the ghost faded, Shane stretched out a hand. "Wait," he pleaded, his voice breaking. "Please."

"Farewell... Lorcan..."

His heart almost bursting, Shane watched as Bres' form began to evaporate into nothingness. "Wait," he cried, "If you are my Dad, where is my mother?"

As the word mother bounced against the cave walls, then echoed and faded, Shane shot bolt upright.

There!

The glowing silhouette of a young woman had materialised and was drifting into view, her slender arms extended lovingly towards Bres' barely discernible form. Her long golden hair was held in a white headband, inlaid with patterns of interconnecting green circles. Her whole body was formed and she seemed to be solid and fixed, glowing as if from some light source deep within.

Shane trembled as the realisation struck him like a train. *My mother! My real mother! Emelda. Oh, oh...*

He half ran, half stumbled towards her, both arms outstretched. "Mum, mother," he called, coughing and whimpering, the words catching in his throat. "Please wait, please…"

Until his dying day he knew he'd never forget the next few moments. Almost in slow motion she turned and her eyes grew wider. She smiled, as if, in whatever dimension she existed, she recognised her baby, her child, her son. Rushing forwards, he shouted her name again and tried to envelop her with both arms but only dry air met his fingers.

She's gone – it had to be her, I just know it was her – I almost touched her.

Head in hands, he collapsed against the wall and slid to the floor. For some minutes, confused tears of love and hate, sorrow and joy, rage and contentment, spilled down his cheeks. Shaking with the enormity of it all, he felt crushed beneath the avalanche of emotion and questions.

That was my mother? Is my father Paddy Donnegan? Or is he, or was he, that tormented ghost?

His fists clenched.

No wonder nobody ever mentioned where I'd come from. Did Paddy Donnegan know he wasn't my father? What could he have known about this underworld pit of horrors? I just know that beautiful shining spirit was my mother!

He wanted to lie down and weep for himself, for Bres and Emelda and Finnoula and for the sweet life that he'd taken so much for granted. All ripped apart.

I never realised there was so much pain in the world but somehow I feel better that I know.

Trying to clear his throbbing brain, he wiped his cheeks, stood upright then strode towards the gloomy exit. Kicking the door open, he spat out a mouthful of dust. "I've a score to settle with Indech."

Chapter 13

The rose pinks and dusty golds of the earlier sunset had faded as Sergeant Canny summoned the sniffer dogs, calling off the search for the night. Throughout the day, the local lifeboat had scoured the bays and coves of Clare Island. A flotilla of pleasure skiffs and small fishing craft had searched the outlying and more inaccessible inlets of Clew Bay itself.

A TV-news crew was hogging the bar of the Atlantic Hotel while Zara and Mr Donnegan stared vacantly through the panoramic windows. They sat alone in the narrow vestibule leading to the foyer, their partly-eaten meal long grown cold on the table. Tubs was snoring gently on the adjoining sofa, a bag of Liquorice Allsorts on the armrest. Gathering twilight was blurring everything outside as high-flying Vs of curlew moved towards the mainland.

Zara sighed, sensing Mr Donnegan's inner bleakness. His drink lay untouched but knowing he was ready to unburden himself, she waited, hands demurely folded across her lap. *Anyone watching us staring outwards could be forgiven for thinking we hadn't a care in the world except soaking up peaceful scenery. Instead of being plonked here like a pair of useless statues, we should be doing something useful…* "Shane's a brilliant swimmer, Mr Donnegan," Zara blurted, "so I don't think he's drowned or anything…"

"He's gone, Zara," muttered Mr Donnegan, almost to himself. "Just like Finnoula, God rest her soul." He paused. "She was floored when those doctors told her she couldn't have children; all she ever wanted was a clatter of the little squealers around the house." He knocked back a large mouthful of whiskey. "First they put her on those nerve tablets. Then it was psychiatrists. She'd be

OK for a while, then she'd fall back into that pit of despair. A shadow of herself is what she became – you can *see* a shadow all right but you can't talk to a shadow; know what I mean?"

Zara nodded emphatically.

"I finally brought her over here to Dad's place, hoping the change of scenery would help. As soon as any of the local kids dropped by, back would come her depression. Oh, she'd smile and everything but it was all a sham. She was eating hardly anything, poor thing..."

He drained his glass and set it down in one swift movement. Zara could see the tremor in his fingers.

"We came back to the cottage one night to find Dad had suffered a stroke and had been taken to A & E. Hearing a loud whingeing outside, I go out and there on the doorstep is a basket with a young baby in it. Nobody else around. Then I saw the note with old fashioned, squiggly writing. It said the baby's parents had recently died in an accident; the Donnegans wanted a child so the baby in the basket was ours if we so wished! Money would be sent for the boy's upbringing and no questions would be asked. No signature; nothing."

"What did you do with the, er, child?" asked Zara, her eyes wide.

"He's my son."

"*What?* Shane is an, an *orphan*?"

"If I ever mentioned where the lad came from, that funny old look of Finnoula's would return so I never brought it up. She was the mother, end of story. Dad passed away soon after and Finnoula, God rest her soul, died from meningitis a few years later."

Only the collapsing embers in the fireplace disturbed the ensuing silence.

"But... didn't Social Services ask or...?"

"…Nobody ever bothered us. We moved to Dublin and kept to ourselves…"

"…But who pays Shane's school fees?" whispered Zara.

"Someone regularly tops up my bank account – how else could I afford Brisbane High or St Columbanus on fisherman's wages…" His voice broke.

"Oh, Mr Donnegan!" Impulsively, Zara put her arms around him. "There, there." She suddenly straightened and pulled away. "I remember now," she cried, a hand covering her mouth.

He blinked. "Remember what?"

"I told you I couldn't recall anything about what happened to the three of us on the beach, yeah?"

"Yes, yes."

"Well, something's coming back. I'm not even sure whether it's a dream…" She closed her eyes, a picture of concentration. "Poly…, er," she mumbled. "Or was it Polyphey-something…?"

She clapped her hands in a sudden blaze of recognition. "Polyphemog! That's what he said his name was. He had a stumpy sword and was huge and muscly." She fell silent as if having difficulty accepting what her memory was telling her then focused on Mr Donnegan's face, half expecting him to laugh. "He had one great eye in the middle of his forehead," she blurted. "He kept telling me to sleep, to forget. He must've hypnotised me. Tubs as well. Mr Donnegan, what's wrong?"

Mr Donnegan was half out of his chair, but still grasping the armrests. "It was a…" he hesitated, then burst out, "…it was a one-eyed man who brought Shane in that basket."

"*What*! But you said that you saw nobody?"

"Only you mentioned a man with a huge single eye, I would've never remembered a thing. He gave no name. I must've been hypnotised too. What's happening to me? It's all come flooding back. Everything is so different from what I thought…"

"…Post-hypnotic suggestion."

Mr Donnegan and Zara swung around. Having overheard their conversation, Tubs was looking intently in their direction.

"What did you say, Finbar?"

"Any hypnotist worth his salt can wipe out part of your memory or make you remember somethin' that never happened; called post-hypnotic suggestions. But they're a bit dodgy and may only last for a short while. Shocks screw up post-hypnotic suggestions. I reckon Shane's disappearance blotted out yours so it's only now you're rememberin' what really happened, Mr D."

"Sit back in your chair, Mr Donnegan," said Zara. "Take your time. Really think… Concentrate…"

Chapter 14

After a long silence, gaunt-faced Paddy Donnegan raised his gaze and began to speak again, this time in troubled, measured tones, as if he wasn't sure of what to say. Or how to say it.

"Yes, yes, yes, I remember – it wasn't the crying of a baby I heard outside, it was somebody banging on the door..." He fell silent, his face puckered, pressing a finger and thumb into the corners of his eyes.

Zara clasped his arm. "Please Mr Donnegan, try and remember what really went down that day."

"Yeah, Mr D, concentrate like hell."

Mr Donnegan remained silent, staring at the wall. His face was pale and he avoided looking directly at Zara and Tubs, as if they weren't there.

"The night was dark and squally," he continued, "as I opened the front door. Standing there in the gloom stood the biggest man I'd ever laid eyes on. His head and face were covered in a cloak and he reminded me of an old fashioned actor in a pantomime or something. Under his massive arm he carried a wickerwork crib, partially covered with a blanket."

"'Where is your father?' this stranger asked. "No hello or how-are-you sort of thing, I could see he was nervous. As I started to explain about Dad's stroke, the stranger interrupted. 'I have little time,' he said. 'All contact between your society and mine is forbidden. I would not have come here were it not my final resort. There are those who would never rest until the young life in this basket is extinguished. I have been tasked with the dying breath of one I hold most dear to ensure this boy's safety. Your father was a good, brave stalwart. I trusted him.'"

"Dad never mentioned…"

'…Many years ago, during a storm, your father dragged me unconscious from the sea. He nursed me back to health. We made an agreement not to tell of our encounter. I have not spoken of it until this day. I feel true sorrow to hear of his sickness. He was the only man of your race I have ever known. My hope is that his great qualities are inherent in you.'

"Look," I said, "I'm finding it hard to understand what you are going on about…"

'…Will you adopt this child?'

"Are you out of your tree?" I said. "It's impossible for…"

'…Look at what I offer you.'

"As he uncovered the basket, his cloak fell back and you could've knocked me down; this guy had only one colossal eye in the middle of his brow! The baby suddenly woke and began to howl the house down.

'Who's crying?' came Finnoula's shout as she ran from the kitchen. Seeing the baby she beamed, lifted it from the basket and rubbed her nose against its forehead. The crying stopped immediately.

She smiled up at the stranger, oblivious to his massive eye. 'Whoever you are, God bless you!' she said."

Mr Donnegan's gaze switched to Tubs then back to Zara before continuing. "I hadn't seen Finnoula smile like that for weeks and I'd already had a bellyful of letters from the adoption people; forms, interviews, references. It was also out of the question to even think of taking someone else's child until the stranger said, 'No other soul will know of this. Your Vow of Never-Speak will be required. Do you agree to our contract?'

"As I stood there flummoxed, Finnoula interrupted, saying," 'I think this little man needs changing.'

With that, she took the nappies from the basket and marched off without a backward glance, cuddling the baby. The stranger pointed to the empty basket and said, 'In there you will find gold, toys and a ring for the boy. You will receive payments until he grows to manhood. Now let us finalise our agreement.'

"'Who are you?' I blurted."

'Do not distress yourself with irrelevant concerns,' he answered. 'I am a true friend of your father. I live nearby. That is all you need to know.'

"I was beginning to panic about the whole thing and saw the stranger's face cloud as I asked, *What if Finnoula can't handle the baby?*'"

'She will return the child within three days to the Scaen Gate on Clare Island at low tide.'

"'The what?' I asked."

'The Scaen Gate… I have marked it on the map which I have placed inside the hiding place.'

"What hiding place?"

'Where I leave items for your father.'

"What items? Where?"

"He pointed to the lintel. 'Behind the eye,' he said."

"Will I ever see you again?"

'No. Now you must stare into my eye…'

"That was the last thing I heard the stranger say."

Blowing out his cheeks, Mr Donnegan fell silent then added, "Everything is as clear as daylight now, but for all those years I remembered nothing. Nothing. The stranger obviously hypnotised Finnoula and me. But there are still so many blanks. How is it possible I recall all this…now…? Finbar is right, it's the shock of Shane's disappearance that's opened up my memory."

The hush was palpable as his voice trailed off and he slumped against the backrest. Nobody had turned on the vestibule lights and all three seemed unaware they were sitting in virtual darkness.

Zara broke the spell by standing up. "Mr Donnegan, you were hypnotised by one of these Clare Island creatures, same with me and Tubs. Probably Shane as well. Shouldn't we go to the police?"

"And tell them Shane's been captured by a giant one-eyed troll? We'd be laughed off the island or be prime suspects in a murder investigation."

"Hey, Mr D, what if the One-Eye that Zara and me met was the same creature that hypnotised you?"

"Creature? It's not right to call him that, Finbar. He may have looked very different but he was definitely a man, of sorts, and a decent one at that. He sounded well-educated... He gave no name..."

"What about One-Eye's map of Clare Island, Mr D – showing the Scaen Gate?"

"I never saw any map, Finbar."

"Didn't your guy say he hid it inside the carvin' over the door?"

As Mr Donnegan scratched his ear, Zara cried, "The wooden eye over Granddad's front door. Bet nobody's ever been near it." She punched a fist into her palm. "Let's go check it out."

Mr Donnegan was already rummaging for the boat keys. "If we find that map, I'll swing *Faith* around and we can be back here on the island before the morning search kicks off. Oh, no!"

"What's wrong, Mr Donnegan?"

"It's far too dark to cross..."

Zara's hands were on her hips. "There's a full moon out, right? Tubs and I will sit on the front of the boat and using the big light that's in the cabin we'll guide you into Granddad's mooring. It's a piece of cake, come on."

"Are you sure, Zara? I mean…"

"…Stop yakking, Mr Donnegan." She elbowed Tubs. "Get moving, dozy; back to the eye."

Chapter 15

Elatha ran towards Shane as he strode through the exit of the House of Hades. Behind her slouched two less than friendly Cyclopes.

"Are you hurt?" she demanded, angry and tired and relieved all at the same time. She rubbed blotches of grime from his face then checked him out for fresh wounds. "Nobody of sane mind enters *that* place. When I saw you had taken the wrong stairway I was afraid to follow you…"

"…What is that place, Elatha?"

She didn't answer immediately but continued to scan his changed, ravaged appearance. "That's where our ancestors' ashes are stored." She shuddered. "We keep far away from…"

"…What's a Watcher?"

Shane saw her hesitate and sensed her discomfort.

"They are, er, special guards who protect us, usually a noble or, less often, a Cyclops. They sometimes spend time in the Up-World."

"I thought Fomorians had nothing to do with the Up-World?"

"Watchers maintain watch on the entry gates but make emergency visits when we are in need of medicine or spare parts. Blending into the Up-World by wearing the correct clothing, they do not appear out of place. Naturally, we don't very often send Cyclopes out." She tittered nervously. "Why this sudden interest in the Watchers?"

"I want to know more about them."

"They are people of honour who will lay down their lives to protect our kingdom."

So the Chief Watcher had been – my father? "Who was Bres?' he asked abruptly.

"He was King Tethra's only son, he…"

"…What happened to him?"

"No more questions," she answered, pointing at the two approaching armed Cyclopes. "Not even *they* will enter the House of Death. They are here to take you to your trial; it is set for this evening."

One of the guards held Shane's arm. The touch was almost friendly. "Car-at-ty boy, I take you to the room of court."

"Nice to meet up again, Polycrates."

"Move," ordered the second Cyclops.

Shane recognised Polyphemog's scowl.

***

Standing in the entrance and flanked by the Cyclopes, Shane surveyed the courtroom. Set in a spacious round chamber, stark walls rose on every side, becoming lost in shadow in the gloom above his head. Whether the expansive grotto had been shaped by Fomorian hands or was just another concavity gouged out by the lava, he was unable to tell. The numerous wall-torches cast wavering shadows across the rows of packed spectators. Alternating pairs of crossed spears and shields lined the walls, each emblazoned with a family name. A long table, sitting on a high podium, dominated the gallery.

"All rise," came a booming voice.

Shane held his breath as the hunched figure of King Tethra shuffled in from a side entrance. He sat on the throne at the head of the table, his grey beard resting against his chest.

Could this frail old man really be my… grandfather? Other than Connaing and Elatha, there's nobody in this place who cares a sneeze about me…

The councillors, clad in purple, filed in behind the king and took their places at the table in descending order of importance. Behind each official, a uniformed standard-bearer stood, an embossed shield shaped in the figure of 8 in one hand, an upright javelin in the other. In front of the king's table, a line of armed Cyclop spearmen stood at ease, facing the dour crowd that was rapidly filling the foreground of the courtroom.

Shane watched as a servant poured wine into the monarch's golden goblet. Having barely tasted the contents, the king handed the receptacle to the adjacent Indech who refused the drink, dismissively passing it on. To polite applause, a bard stepped forward, bowed to the king and following a slow introduction on his harp, began to recite. Indech sat impassively at the king's side throughout and as the bard departed, pressed coins into his hand.

"Legal proceedings will now commence," a councillor called.

Indech was first to his feet and his opening remarks were brisk and businesslike. "Welcome, Your Majesty. I went to great pains to see you were not disturbed but the illustrious Minister of Culture insisted you be taken from your sickbed. The issue is simple; in spite of all our efforts, an Up-Worlder has violated our domain, hence our laws must be applied and the invader executed forthwith. Thank you, Your Majesty."

Shane felt ice flow through his veins as Connaing rose with slow deliberation, right thumb hooked into his toga, left hand resting on the table. Connaing remained silent for some moments, staring ahead before speaking. "Your Majesty, we have a boy in our midst, here by freak accident. Execution of invaders applies only to those of mature years. We Fomorians are a proud race, our laws must be vigorous but fair. I hold this youngster should be spared, hence my request for a full Council meeting."

The king strained forward. "Bring forth the prisoner."

As the two Cyclopes frogmarched Shane through the crowd and stood by his side as he faced the bench, the king mumbled, "The boy is of tender years."

"This is a court of law, sire," said Indech softly, his tone almost conversational, "a place for cold legal decisions, not sentiment. The invader's age is of no consequence, it is the futures of *our* children that must remain foremost in the minds of this court. We have only survived because of strong and binding laws, otherwise we would fare no better than the Up-World we shun."

Shane felt his insides turn to jelly as a murmur of approval swept through the assembly.

"Should our existence even be suspected by outsiders," continued Indech affably, "then our society is no more. The fact that your own son was drowned, sire, may be weakening your resolve to apply the law to one so young. I therefore entreat you to make the right decision and order an immediate execution. Thank you, sire."

Fighting back a sob, Shane looked wildly around the sea of faces. *Nobody is even looking at me; I don't matter; I don't exist; this is too much to take...*

The king addressed Connaing. "If the young one is pardoned, he must spend the rest of his days among us. He might escape, no matter how alert our security. Indech informs me that we are besieged by boats searching for this captive."

"I would take all responsibility for the *boy*, Your Majesty. He can reside with my family and..."

Indech interrupted smoothly, "...Our continued existence hangs on a knife edge, sire. Such risks are unacceptable, you must know this. I urge you, make the right judgement."

"This is far too painful a decision for an old man," mumbled the king. "I give leave to our six councillors to decide by a show of hands."

The court recorder rose and declared, "The king has spoken; those for executing the invader..."

Shane's heart was hammering against his ribcage. *Maybe one or two councillors will feel sorry for me or something? Perhaps Connaing spoke to them earlier on my behalf? What if somebody abstains? What if...*

Indech's hand was already aloft with two other councillors.

"Those for sparing the invader..." continued the recorder.

Connaing's palm rose accompanied by two others.

Three! The vote is tied! I'm saved! Or am I...?

Indech's long robes swished as he rose and raised his hand in saluting the king. "You, sire, have the casting vote. For all our sakes, sire, use it wisely."

Tethra's frame seemed to shrink further as his tortured eyes fell on Shane. "I don't always agree with you, or your methods, Indech, but the safety of our people must always be my prime concern." He hesitated, his arthritic hands trembling as he gripped the table. "With great sadness, I decree that the boy must die." Blinking erratically he added, "Matters such as these do neither my body nor soul any good. I return to my sickbed."

People are shouting. Cheering. Elatha is crying in the front row. Am I back in a new version of my nightmare? My knees feel wobbly...

Stunned and frozen in fear, Shane saw Indech's teeth flash in the torchlight as he addressed Connaing.

"I told you I would win, dancer of jigs," he cried triumphantly. To the guards he shouted, "Take the Up-Worlder back to jail. He's for the pool tomorrow."

Chapter 16

"WAIT!"

Shane's impassioned yell stunned the court. He knew young Fomorians rarely spoke unless spoken to; addressing a court unbidden would be unheard of. "Your Majesty – I cannot be guilty of invading your kingdom."

"Be silent," said Indech softly. "You are an outsider."

"No," Shane said. "I'm a Fomorian!"

All I've got going for me now is the truth and a few precious seconds of surprise. Maybe just enough time to make my case before I'm manhandled back to the cells.

"My name is Lorcan, Your Majesty," he called out directly to the king. "I am your grandson."

Nobody moved or spoke. In that momentary lull, the king halted in mid step and turned to stare, his initial shock soothed somewhat by Shane's humble tone. Indech leapt from the table, his finger pointing like a pistol but before he could speak, Shane cried, "I am the son of Bres. Look, my royal ring."

He stretched his arm high into the air, allowing the gold to glint in the torchlight. The court was in uproar. All councillors were standing, talking and gesticulating at the same time. Below, those seated on stools had also shot to their feet, shouting, arguing, waving their arms. As the monarch grasped the table, Indech pounded the wood with his fist.

"Order," he shouted. "This court will come to ORDER. Polyphemog, what of that ring?"

The Cyclops marched forward and grabbed Shane's hand. "It as he say," came the grunted reply. "Fomorian ring."

Indech's smile widened. "Sire, our laws state that any child produced by the union of a Fomorian and an outsider must be put to death. I well knew Bres had married some milkmaid from the Island but never realised he had smuggled his new-born infant into our kingdom. This child's existence was known only to Connaing." His voice dropped. "Our respected Minister of Culture secretly handed the mongrel child to Up-Worlders for adoption. This is double treason – a crime punishable by death."

Whatever little colour had been in the king's face had faded. "Is this true, Connaing?" he whispered. "How can this boy be related to me and I not be informed of his very existence? What is happening?"

Straining every nerve to follow the exchanges, Shane switched his attention to Connaing who stood motionless and silent. *Come on, Connaing, it's down to you; you're my only hope...*

With every facial muscle taut, Connaing eventually spoke. "Your Majesty, your son confided in me that he had taken a wife but never did he mention the existence of a child so it was not I who gave Bres' infant to Up-Worlders. You were in your sickbed, therefore I decided to keep Bres' return a secret, until you recovered. I considered it best..."

"*You* considered it *best,*" Indech interrupted, his tone still friendly. He strode across the court to stand in front of Connaing. "Your selfish decision jeopardised our race," he continued softly. "Sadly, we cannot afford a conniving minister who conspires against the interests of his own people. I respectfully request, Your Majesty, that Connaing be eradicated forthwith." He smiled. "He should have been eradicated years ago."

Shane's heart sank as the druid retook his place and the court buzzed. *Indech has won. The crowd are behind him. What a monster...*

A councillor was on his feet. "Let us rid ourselves of the troublesome newcomer. Connaing the traitor likewise."

Another hollered, "Indech is right; execute the contemptible pair. They will only bring further trouble on our heads. Take a vote, now."

The court recorder, hands in the air for silence, called, "All those who decree Connaing's death, raise your hands!"

Five councillors' hands rose.

As Tethra buried his face in his hands, Indech called, "The Council has decided. By rights, Connaing's body should be fed to the sharks but out of respect for his loyal ancestors, I shall allow his ashes to be stored in the House of Armour. The Up-Worlder's body will be loosed into the tide; all needless activity around the Island will cease when his corpse is found. This session is now ended."

No! No! No! Not as long as I can draw my breath is this ended!

As Indech reached for his gavel, Shane's shout electrified the gathering. "INDECH, YOU ARE A KILLER."

His face ablaze, Shane was striding towards the table, his right index finger pointing at the druid.

"You, sir," he articulated loudly, hoping that his words would make their mark, "drowned my father and my mother." The pulse pounding in his ears was now so loud he could barely hear his own voice. Staring into Indech's eyes he added, "They were given no trial. It was murder." He was taken aback to see that Indech betrayed no emotion, other than smiling.

"This court has no interest in your rantings," Indech said matter-of-factly. He waved an arm towards the exit. "March him to the cells."

"Hold," wheezed the king, tottering unsteadily to his feet. "I wish to hear what this boy has to say."

White-faced, Shane now stood directly below the council table, knowing that any chance of survival depended on his next few sentences.

"Thank you, Your Majesty, noble grandfather," he began with as much courtesy as he could muster. "Indech murdered my parents. As a Fomorian, I have a right to speak."

As the full significance of his words sank in, he could see that many in the hushed courtroom had been swayed by his openness and fierce conviction.

Indech threw his head back. "Me? A murderer?" he said with a soft, dismissive laugh. "Ramblings and nonsense. This court has heard enough jabbering from a desperate prisoner trying to save his skin."

The king spoke, a sudden sharpness in his voice. "But you have not answered the charges this boy makes, Indech."

"Laughable charges, sire. I, in my official capacity, had your guilty son and his illicit wife taken care of. Bres openly admitted his treason; you were in a coma from your fall and I wished to spare you the pain of overseeing a trial and execution. It was unanimously decided that you be told the pair had accidentally drowned. Reopening these old wounds is weakening you. Would that you had been protected from these unsavoury theatrics."

Indech is winning him over; how can the king swallow all those lies? I must get my oar in before the opportunity passes...

"You also stole my father's ring," interrupted Shane, his voice louder and insistent. "You use it to braid your hair."

Indech pointed to the exit. "Take them both to the cells."

The king weakly raised a hand. "Indech, I have just learned how my only son died. I am distraught. You did not inform me. I was told nothing, nothing…" He paused. "Settle this current matter to my satisfaction. I demand to view whatever object plaits your hair."

The corners of Indech's mouth twitched. "Sire," he protested, "I will not be treated as common riff-raff…"

"…Guards; expose what fastens this man's hair."

Before the sentries moved, Connaing lunged and with his free hand wrenched back Indech's hood. Close to the skull, amid the greasy black hair, a ring secured the druid's ponytail. As a guard held a spear against Indech's jugular, Connaing slid the golden band free and held it under the glow of the nearby torch.

"The inscription on the ring reads, *AITEAMH*," he said.

Almost in a trance, the king slumped back onto the throne, his body shaking. "It is the Ring of Persuasion. I myself bestowed it on, on… my poor, poor son…"

Chapter 17

Shane blinked, trying to make sense of the sudden confusion. Amid the movements of shouting spectators and gesticulating officials, Indech had shaken himself free of Connaing's grip and was flanked by Cyclopes with upright shields and drawn swords, three to his left, three to the right. Two others, dressed in similar military fatigues, were half dragging, half walking Connaing towards the exit.

Indech's troops are appearing from nowhere. They're beating up those two councillors who voted for me; they've blocked the exits; the place is surrounded.

Marching in time, Indech's six Cyclopes were forcibly brushing aside anyone in their path, shielding and protecting him as he strode across the court. On reaching the king's bench, he raised his arms and stood before the assembly, a new maniacal fierceness settling over his features. Shane could feel matters were quickening; strange and dangerous emotions were in the air.

"My people, I ask that you all come to order," Indech calmly announced.

As the druid completed his first sentence, Shane saw him nonchalantly reach out and take the Ring of Persuasion from the table and slip it on his finger.

"My whole existence," he continued, "has been devoted to your protection. King Tethra is seriously ill; he leaves no heir and stubbornly refuses to nominate one. We must stop looking to the past – to our defeated ancestors, to the Therians, the Tuatha de Dannan, the Tomb People – bygones all – we must prepare for the future."

Shane noticed the silence settling over the unruly public gallery; an unnatural, uncanny hush. Similarly, the benches and workplaces of the councillors, elders, officials and scribes; all those either seated or standing appeared fixated, their faces rapt, hyperattentive, gazing at Indech.

Shane became aware of soft waves percolating through his own body. Suffused with this new warm contentment, he felt both sleepy and alert at the same time. *Maybe I was wrong about Indech, he's actually speaking a lot of sense...*

"...It is time for a new leader who will place *your* concerns first. I control the Cyclopes, our army, finances and production systems, so I ask you all now to come to my call. We must all move together towards a glorious, more secure destiny."

He really does sound like a man for the future; someone you could trust...

"My ancestors ensured our survival after the Tuatha de Dannan's trickery drove us underground. Down here we've withstood all invaders – Viking, Norman, English – because we've remained tightknit, unseen and resolute. We have avoided the abominations of the Up-World; the widespread destruction of the planet, societies eaten away by the woodworms of drugs, violence, greed and corruption."

He really understands what's going on. I'm a Fomorian; he gets my vote, does Indech. Any day.

Shane shook his head viciously. *INDECH IS NICE!? What am I thinking?*

He took in the silent gathering. More carefully this time...*What's happening – the audience looks weird. It's got to be that Ring of Indech's that has me thinking like this. It's working on everyone else. I must remain focused; alert; I mustn't let that Ring's power work on me.*

As he instinctively massaged his own ring, Shane felt the druid's eyes fall on him.

"…Up-World children do not understand the word respect. Have we not already witnessed today's display of despicable manners and wholesale lies by this trespasser? Would any of you here allow one of your children to speak with such insolence?"

Shane heard the angry murmur sweep through the assembly.

"We make do without luxuries and we live for our common cause. We know what to expect from our Up-World enemies. Because they are different, our Cyclopes would be hounded into zoos. We will only remain safe if we adapt to meet the new challenges, throw aside the old ways so to be better prepared to defend the last of the Fomorians. Vote for me or vote for collapse, corruption and captivity. Decide."

Shane remained riveted; he'd never witnessed such a monstrously clever and passionate performance. He was baffled at how effective and powerful Indech's speech had been. As he caught sight of Elatha's tear-stained face in the crowd, loud cheering erupted throughout the chamber followed by mass applause. A chorus of "INDECH, INDECH," rang out, accompanied by rhythmic foot stamping and clapping.

Indech acknowledged the accolade, his voice smooth as treacle. "Good people, you have chosen well. The time is ripe for the old to depart."

Shane watched spellbound as Indech half turned towards Tethra and smiling ruefully, proffered his hand, as if acknowledging an opponent who'd mounted a brave but losing defence at the chessboard. The king didn't respond but remained staring vacantly ahead.

"My only son *murdered*," he sobbed. "Monumental treachery."

"There, there, King Tethra," tutted Indech sympathetically, "or should I say, ex-king Tethra. You are deposed. Collect your possessions and remove yourself to the Cyclopes' quarters." He smiled. "Should I hear a squeak of protest from you or any of your pampered circle, I will have your throats slit."

The king buried his face in his hands.

Indech signalled to the bodyguards. "Take this creature to his new accommodation." Addressing the crowd he shouted, "The king has abdicated. He has named me his successor. I, Indech, am your new leader."

Shane listened as further cheering echoed around the courtroom while stools and shields were overturned as people milled forwards to shake Indech's hand. Others moved to the side, shaking their heads, flabbergasted at what was happening. A few advanced to pay their final respects to the hunched Tethra but were unceremoniously driven away by the Cyclopes.

"Guards," called Indech. "I shall be along to the cells presently to 'interrogate' Connaing before his morning swim. Take the Up-Worlder to the pool for immediate execution."

Shane took two steps towards Indech. "Please, sir, can I say goodbye to Elatha?"

Indech allowed himself a little razor-blade of a smile. "Sadly, no," he answered with mock sympathy. "You came into this world alone and so you shall leave it."

Chapter 18

Shane shivered again.

I'm going to die. I've done nothing... this is so wrong... He fought against his helpless rage... *I'm so alone...*

Wrists bound and dwarfed by two armed Cyclopes, he stood at the edge of the Execution Pool, confused and tortured by the certainty of his imminent death. He stared vacantly into the black water, fighting the overriding feelings of terror and doom that threatened to drive him sobbing to his knees. He was past tears.

"I sorry for these troubles, Car-at-ty Boy."

Realising that one of the Cyclopes was actually speaking to him, Shane became aware of the vaguely familiar face gazing down at him, compassion radiating from the eye.

"Er, thanks, Polycrates. It's not your fault."

"You be too young but I cannot help about...." He inclined his head towards the pool.

"When do I... when do I go in...?"

"In ten minute. Jail man bringing execution stones for feet."

Less than a quarter of an hour of my life left! Will my last memories be of horror, fish ponds, cave walls, rock...

"Stop! Now!"

He swung around to see Elatha running over the uneven terrain towards the pool, her long hair flowing. Panting, she came to a standstill in front of Polycrates and pushed a single sheet of green paper into his hand.

"Shay-An has been pardoned," she cried. "Indech has changed his mind so he is ordered back to the courtroom. NOW!"

Polycrates remained staring blankly at the official-looking document.

Elatha whipped it from his grasp. "Look," she said with desperate conviction, talking and jabbing the sheet at the same time. "Shay-An's pardon is signed by Indech himself. What is the problem; can't you see for yourself?"

Polycrates was rubbing his forehead. "Me cannot read, no understand this, this…"

"…Well, Polycrates, *I* can read and *I* can understand and *I* can tell you that if Shay-An is not brought back this instant then…" Her voice dropped as she pointed dramatically. "It's *you* and your friend who'll end up in that pool, not Shay-An." Hands on hips, she glared upward into the single eye. "You'd better get a move on."

Polycrates turned to show the document to his equally baffled companion. Heads close together and obviously troubled, they placed their swords on the ledge and moved away, conversing in short, terse whispers.

Her eyes blazing, Elatha grabbed Shane's arm. "I forged that pardon, so listen," she whispered fiercely, her nails biting into his flesh. "On the way back we pass Eochu's statue. There I drop my water gourd. Behind the statue lies a narrow cleft. Wide enough for a body to fit through. Lugh and I used play hide-and-find there. You will have the shortest of time to squeeze past. I shall be behind you. A Cyclops is too wide to pass through…."

"…Oh, Elatha, you're… I'm so glad to see you… I…."

She placed a finger over his lips. "…Ssh, they return. Remember, this is our only chance."

Polycrates spoke slowly. "We not understand writing like this but we take Car-at-ty Boy back. Stay close."

The second Cyclops hitched his shield without speaking and slouched sullenly behind Elatha, sword in hand.

Shane was still trying to get his head around Elatha's plan when the narrow passageway opened into a wider thoroughfare, dominated by a thin, five metre column of naturally-formed limestone. Set a little back from the pathway on a slight incline, a bust of Eochu sat on top of the slab. With Polycrates in the lead and the second guard to the rear, Shane scanned the structure but could discern no hidden aperture. Fighting his crushing disappointment he continued to stare and took a sharp intake of breath. *There!* Not a gap, more a narrow strip of blackness. An indistinct shadow of hope.

"Please, Polycrates," called Elatha. "May I drink?"

Reluctantly the leading Cyclops stopped as Elatha rummaged in her sack for the water bottle. Shane, feigning weariness, leaned against Eochu's memorial. The long slit was out of sight except to the keenest eye.

"My water is stale, Polycrates," said Elatha. "Perhaps I can have some of yours?"

As he laid down his shield, and removed his shoulder sack, Elatha's bottle hit the ground and rolled past the second Cyclops. Instinctively he bent down but failed to grasp the container as it rolled down the incline. He swore.

Both guards are distracted. NOW!

One bound took Shane behind Eochu's column. Refusing to allow himself to make the slightest sound, he compressed his bound wrists into his groin, flattened his shoulders then squeezed through, barely scraping his knees in the process. What he hadn't bargained for was Elatha's speed. Coming so close on his heels, she crashed into him as she shouldered her body through the crevice, sending them both tottering. His lined features creased into the semblance of a smile as he heard the Cyclopes' howls of rage as the irate guards realised they could neither catch nor pursue their quarry.

"Thanks, Elatha," Shane panted, as she unknotted his ropes. He held her face in his trembling hands. "You were brill, brill. What a great plan; I…"

"…Please keep moving, Shay-An."

With the musty stink of staleness in his nostrils, Shane followed her along the unlit, low-ceilinged passageway. Sporadic shafts of light from above meant they didn't have to walk in total darkness. A loud shriek sounded somewhere in the distance, followed by a series of screams.

"Shay-An, we are now close to the courtroom. We…"

"Then I must help Connaing," he cried. "He's twice saved my life."

Her voice shook. "Have you taken leave of your senses? You will be speared within seconds. We must find a safe place to hide."

"I can't leave your father…"

"…This is civil war, Indech is destroying all those who stand against him. No one is safe. Make haste."

He could hear the distant sound of marching feet and the clink of arms. Another harrowing howl of pain from a passageway close by made him wince. It seemed as if every Fomorian was on the move, running or jostling through the maze of passages and the alleyways that now echoed with the shouts and cries of very angry men.

"What's that?"

As if to answer him, a fresh bout of clashing swords and swearing sounded very close, followed by a man's tearful whimpering.

Elatha's eyes were wide. "Neighbour is now against neighbour; taking revenge."

"Elatha, wait."

"No stopping."

He restrained her with both hands. "Please, we must head back to your house."

"Why return there?"

"First I need my jeans and trainers and your dad's holding some stuff of mine."

"What is stuff?"

"Don't worry about it, just take me there."

"You irritate me with your secrets."

"Look, we're going to need food and water; yeah?"

She pondered. "Yes, yes… you are right, we'll need sustenance for a long journey."

"How long?"

"Many leagues of unexplored caves lead from here; we can avoid Indech for weeks, months. But we must keep to the unfrequented passageways. Longer but safer."

It seemed to Shane they'd been trudging forever before he saw the distant pinpoint of light. *A way out!* As the exit drew closer, Elatha raised a warning finger. The cramped opening lay two metres above the narrow thoroughfare where Connaing's house stood. She peeked through like an inquisitive woodpecker then signalled him forward.

"I fancy getting my hands on something to defend ourselves with," he grunted.

Taking her hand, Shane moved forwards, every nerve in his body alert. Hardly daring to breathe and crouching low, he circled the silent house twice, then reconnoitered the gardens. He looked through each open window then checked for the presence of another being. Or an upstairs ambush.

All normal.

The street lay in gloom as he pushed aside the entrance drape. Back against the wall, he held his breath, listening for any normal household sound – a chair being lifted, a rustle or a creak of movement...

Nothing.

"Mother?" Elatha called softly, standing outside the kitchen.

No answer.

Shane surveyed the lower floor and kitchen then signaled Elatha to ascend the stairway close on his heels. He mounted the stairs on tiptoe, entered the sleeping quarters and first rummaged in the wooden chest beside Connaing's bed. Next he ran his fingers through batches of clothing, chucking garments aside as he ransacked each cubbyhole. More in desperation than anything else, he opened the small shaving stand and grunted. There it was, together with his watch, torch and wallet.

He made for the landing holding the metallic object above his head.

"What are you holding, Shay-An?" Elatha whispered.

"My mobile, fully charged. I'm going to call the police. Then Dad to..."

"...No! Your father yes, but never the Up-World police! We would be invaded by..."

"...OK, OK, but look, I can contact whoever I want by just pressing these buttons..."

"...I am aware of the workings of a mobile phone," she replied coldly.

"Oops, sorry. This is Dad's old phone. I'm saving to buy the latest update with all the gizmos..."

"Gis mos?"

His smile froze as he switched off the torch.

They both remained absolutely still, hearing the bump downstairs of a body knocking against something solid.

Someone had come through the rear door and was moving about. Shane spotted the glint of light at the edge of the stairway. *Someone's torch? Yes. How many people? Doesn't matter, any is too many. We're trapped! What can we do? Nothing. Wait.* He held a finger up for silence, listening hard. Close to the stairs, two shadows moved inside the room under his feet.

The first person whispered. "Nobody's down here. I told you they couldn't be that stupid."

The second person. "You search upstairs; I'll take the gardens."

Both Shane and Elatha's mouths flew open. *Lugh!* Plus one companion.

There's two of them, at least. I'm going to have to fight my way out of this; no other way.

Bracing himself, he heard the soft scrape on the upstairs landing. Until then, the person hadn't made a sound but paused before pushing the bedroom drape aside. The light from the downstairs torch cast the intruder's shadow on the bedroom wall.

A tall, hunched figure; a weapon of some sort in his right hand.

Shane waited until a silhouette was framed in the doorway then crashed forwards, driving his shoulder into the intruder's midriff. He heard the surprised oomph as the stranger tottered, hit the hallway wall and cascaded backwards down the stairs. Shane winced as he heard bone crunch against wood as the man's head somehow jammed between the banisters of the final step.

"Run, Elatha," he cried.

He cleared the last three steps in one jump then leapt over the still-twitching body. Tearing through the kitchen, he stood erect, pressing his back against the wall of the adjoining storeroom. Trying to regulate his breathing, he remained motionless until he heard Elatha's footfalls on the ground floor.

"Stay a while, dearest sister."

Having come in from the courtyard, Lugh now stood in the kitchen doorway, his back turned towards Shane, his loaded bow primed, the arrow pointing at Elatha.

"One move and you're dead." His tone was matter of fact, almost friendly.

Shane could see by her expression that Elatha was still trying to take everything in. "Are you mad?" she exploded, trying to control both her rage and fear.

Lugh's reply was sweet and reasonable. "May I ask you the same question? Are you not helping the Up-Worlder to escape?"

Careful Elatha, please be careful.

"Shay-An is a Fomorian," said Elatha through gritted teeth. "One of us."

"He is an imposter and a liar."

Shane remained fixated on the arrow tip, knowing Lugh needed only the flimsiest of reasons to release the bowstring.

"What of Indech murdering the king's son?" demanded Elatha. "And father – isn't he speaking the truth?"

"He broke our laws. I am a Warrior Watcher – I didn't choose my parents. I tolerate them."

"I never did understand you."

"Father committed treason, even you can understand that. Because you are my sister, I shall try to ignore your stupidity. But only this one last time."

"And mother?"

"I oversaw her arrest."

Shane watched Elatha's face drain of colour. "You... you arrested your own mother?" he heard her whisper, her voice unrecognisable.

"Rules must be upheld, Elatha dear. Tread carefully, otherwise you might find yourself with her in the pool."

During this exchange, Lugh's eyes never deflected from his target, nor did the tension on the bowstring lessen.

"I am ordered by Indech to dispatch the invader who relies on your help to escape. He cannot be far away. I plan to take him here or hunt him down like the dog that he is. It matters not a jot to me." A semblance of a smile crossed his lips as he made a slight adjustment to the bowstring.

While hanging on to every syllable, Shane was desperately trying to locate something to fight with. Anything would do. Then it struck him; he was standing in the very room where Lugh's battle gear was stored. Seeing the outline of short wooden swords propped against the wall, he grasped the nearest, knowing that Elatha was using all her guile to keep her brother's attention focused elsewhere. He refused to think about what would happen if he couldn't use the weapon quickly enough.

Lugh was talking as Shane lifted the drape and stepped into the torch-lit room.

"...I hold no grudge against you, little sister. Please tell me where the Up-Worlder hides, it is he I wish to kill, not my pretty sister. You would leave me with no choice..."

From the moment he emerged into the open, Shane knew he was hopelessly exposed. It would also take three steps to get within striking distance of Lugh. If Elatha deviated her stare or showed the slightest sign of surprise, then they were both very dead meat indeed – he'd seen more than enough of Lugh's dexterity with knife and bow. He stared unblinkingly at the back of Lugh's head… *From this moment on, everything that happens to me for the rest of my life depends on my not making the slightest mistake...*

Elatha continued to focus unwaveringly on her brother's face as Shane took his second, then his final step, the sword cocked two-handed over his right shoulder. Willing everything into the weapon's downward acceleration, his arms jarred as the heavy wood crashed against flesh and vertebrae. As Lugh collapsed without a sound, the arrow automatically shot from the bow. Elatha jerked her head sideways as it whizzed past, shaving away a string of butter-coloured hair.

Shane remained motionless, continuing to stare sightlessly at the crumpled body at his feet. He knew that concern for Elatha wasn't the sole reason his blow had been so brutal. And effective.

He said hoarsely, "Never turn your back on an enemy, Lugh."

Chapter 19

Shane continued to stare at the two unconscious bodies. He'd dragged both into the hallway where they lay side by side. Lugh's features appeared normal, as if sleeping peacefully while his companion was barely breathing, his face a pallid grey. A trickle of blood ran from his left ear and nose.

"I didn't mean to hurt Lugh's mate more than I had to, Elatha," he said, breaking the long silence.

"Don't you understand? Lugh is out to kill you. And his friend, Manderas – they are favourites of Indech; a ruthless pair. He will be furious when he hears of this."

"First things first. What about water and grub?"

"I've packed fish, potato-cakes, goorama..."

"...Then we must get to the highest possible point in the kingdom."

"Why so?"

"Mobiles don't work well underground. I've switched it off to save power. Same with the torch. Have you a map of the kingdom?"

She shook her head.

"Lugh must've had charts showing the gates and that; he was a Watcher, after all."

"Watchers' work is secret. He forbade me to enter his bedroom."

Shane was already halfway up the stairs, first to grab his jeans and trainers then across the landing into Lugh's room.

Splintering open Lugh's cupboard reminds me of that awful crack Manderas' head made on the stairs. And those dreadful twitching limbs. I've injured a human being! Maybe killed another! I didn't want to but... I might have to do the same again...

Lifting a leather folder from the top shelf, he took a sharp intake of breath. Inside lay a neat wad of parchment maps and charts.

"Got everything we need," he shouted, descending the stairs two at a time. "Exit gates, the lot. Question is, how do we get to the top spot?"

Elatha spread one of the maps across the living room table. "The nearest point to the Up-World is the Hellespont…"

"…The what?"

"It's named after a place in Ancient Greece where…"

"…Yeah, yeah…"

"…But you cannot leave that way. The Gates are the only way out."

"We've gotta try the mobile first."

"But to leave or enter the kingdom, we need to know the times of the tides."

"How come?"

"Because two of our exit doors lie below high-water level."

It wasn't the sort of news he wanted to hear. "Who has all this info?" he asked, quickly slipping on his jeans and trainers.

"The Watchers. Indech. Councillors. Ordinary Fomorians have little interest in…"

"…How far to this Hellespont?"

"It is an arduous journey toward the Catacombs. Little is known about the place. Indech will be searching everywhere else. You are ill-clad for such a trip."

"I'm checking the torch, you take the grub and water." He pointed. "I need those." He bent down to remove Lugh's two daggers and slid them inside his belt.

"Why take Lugh's miodógs?"

"You never know."

The going became more difficult as they penetrated deeper into the bowels of the kingdom. Shane became aware of the rise in temperature and this time there were no adjoining pathways, just crevices to squeeze through, obstacles to surmount and the same monotonous stone everywhere.

***

After a further two hours, the track began to drop steeply then opened into a vaulted cavern. Resembling a gargantuan stone cathedral, it was spacious and full of echoes. High above, resembling giant javelins, elongated stalactites hung from the ceiling, opposed by stunted stalagmites jutting upwards from the floor. Huge boulders lay scattered around, making Shane feel puny and insignificant. The walls were multicoloured; greens, reds, blues, even purples, as if a giant prehistoric artist had once worked them with a colossal paintbrush.

"Let's rest, Elatha."

"I'm weak from hunger," she sighed, opening up her sack.

"Easy on the food; we have to ration it." Although obviously alone, they nonetheless spoke in hushed tones.

"Why are you whispering, Shay-An?"

"It just feels as if…" He glanced around uneasily. "…There's somebody else here."

"Perhaps it is because this place is so vast and we are so small."

"Let's work out where we are."

Shane held the torch as she smoothed out the map on flat rock. "Much further you reckon?"

"Some while yet."

"I'm switching off the torch; the battery's running down."

She tapped her bag. "I've brought Fomorian torches; one made from pitch, the second from dried algae. Both give off strong glows. Let us rest awhile."

Without the flashlight, the darkness was near complete. In the distance somewhere, Shane was aware of a constant dribble of rainwater percolating from the world above. Otherwise only their footfall and small movements disturbed the profound stillness. *How on earth did those earlier Fomorians survive down here?*

"Why do your people live underground?"

Elatha selected a place to sit and leant back, hugging her knees. "Our main concern was to evade the Tuatha De Dannan and other enemies. In later times if we were attacked, the Cyclopes proved to be notable fighters." In the darkness Shane heard her swallow a mouthful of water before continuing. "St. Patrick never attempted to convert the Cyclopes because it was accepted that this island was peopled by giant one-eyed pirates. In the Middle Ages, plague forced us to migrate further underground to keep our existence secret..."

"...Come on," snorted Shane. "You must come across other humans?"

"We have measures to protect us in such circumstances."

"Like?"

"The Cyclopes can hypnotise strangers to blot out the memory of any such encounter."

"Like with Tubs and Zara on the beach?"

"Yes, but it takes time for the eye magic to work. Otherwise recollections could return."

"Can the two-eyed Fomorians hypnotise others?"

"No, we use our mirrors."

"Mirrors?"

"Even though most of us will never brave the Up-World, every Fomorian carries a mirror."

"You too?"

"Always."

He switched on the torch. "Let's have a look."

She removed a small glistening circular object from inside her tunic and handed it over.

"Hey, it made my fingers tingle," he said, running his fingers over the smooth surface.

"Through the centuries our mirror-makers handed down the instructions on how to make them. Under the full moon they boiled down the special seawater and powders from rifts in the seabed where the hot gases escape from the Earth's core. That mirror is five hundred years old. Mirac, our childless mirror-maker, died last year so if I break this, no replacement is available."

"What does it *do?*"

"If someone shines a Formorian mirror into your eyes, the previous five seconds of your life are blotted out. Flash the mirror twice and a longer portion of your memory is wiped away. Following the removal of an Up-Worlder's recent recollections, he or she becomes confused and unsure of what is happening, allowing us plenty of time to disappear." She passed Shane a small package. "Hide this inside your clothing," she said, then flashed the mirror into his eyes, causing him to blink.

After a short pause she quietly asked, "Where is the food I gave you?"

His forehead creased. "What food?"

She laughed behind her hand.

"What's so damned funny, eh?" he said.

Elatha leant over and pulled the bag from his jacket.

"But – how did this get there? I don't remember..."
Comprehension dawned as he met her laughing eyes. He
smiled, shaking his head. "You're a memory-wiper!"

"The mirror is effective at a mile distance so on the
rare occasion that a Watcher might encounter an islander,
he simply uses his mirror." She replaced the mirror in her
tunic. "Enough talking; there are many hills between here
and the Hellespont."

He grinned. "That mirror would come in real handy in
class." His mentioning school brought the memories
flooding back; Tubs and Zara, laughter, messing around
behind the ref's back, the away trips... He deliberately
blocked out anything remotely unpleasant like the cross-
country runs and those hairy call-ups to the Head. *Will I
ever make it back to beautiful normality again?*

Chapter 20

Before Elatha told him their destination was close, he'd become aware of vague draughts of distant fresh air and the odour of moist clay. His spirits rose. In the roof of the widening chamber high above, he saw thin, sporadic shafts of light shining through the tiny fissures in the island's crust. *The Up-World's getting closer.*

They stopped to gulp down water as Shane unfolded the map. In the tiny circle of torchlight, Elatha ran a finger over the parchment, finally pinpointing their position. "Yonder."

"What's yonder?"

"The Hellespont; half an hour's climb. We are unlikely to encounter anyone up there."

Shane's fingernails were broken and chipped, his knees and elbows bruised as the trek led everlastingly uphill. The earlier well-marked trail had long petered out so they had to clamber over rocky spoil or barriers composed of large, irregular crags. Elatha had hardly a scratch. No matter how unpredictable or hazardous the surroundings, she vaulted the most daunting obstacles like a mountain goat.

"How come," he panted, "you just rock'n'roll over everything while I get battered and bruised?"

"I'm top of our climbing class…" she began before suddenly stiffening, finger on her lips. Not daring to move, he watched her motionless figure on the boulder above his head as she strained to identify the strange noise. Then he heard it. A shuffle, followed by a sigh and the sound of a large body starting to move. Then the sound of someone loudly breaking wind. Ten metres away.

A shout. "Amalog, wait."

Cyclopes! Here? Close by, yes, but on the far side of the separating barrier of limestone.

As the footfall faded, Shane shielded his nose.

"Phew," he whispered. "What's that pong?"

"It was a Cyclops going to the release closet, er, the toilet," she hissed.

"First time I ever heard a Cyclops fart."

Despite their perilous situation, Shane sniggered. Attempting to suppress the upwelling giggle, he jammed his hand over his mouth. When Elatha saw his bulging eyes, she doubled up with the same contagious mirth. Whimpering, she slid down along the rock face, biting the inside of her cheeks. Holding their sides, they waited for the fit of hilarity to subside. Which it eventually did.

"Shay-An, you are the silliest, most stupid…"

He wiped away the tears. "Sorry, Elatha, I couldn't help it. I wonder how big a Cyclops' toilet roll is?"

Composing herself sufficiently, Elatha put her hands on her hips and said severely, "That is enough!"

"You're right," gasped Shane, giving her a playful push.

"We use the public toilets. Cyclopes sometimes use the nearest hole in the ground."

She picked up her sack, deliberately not meeting his eye.

***

From ten metres above the deserted passageway, Elatha peered through the gaps between the limestone flags, checking out their new surroundings. On her signal, they slid down the slope and tore across the narrow road. Without breaking stride and at full speed, they began the tortuous climb up the opposite side, making little more noise than shadows. Reaching the topmost edge of smooth rock, they threw themselves down on the flat surface.

Scanning the open map, Shane could feel the excitement surge through his veins as he recognised where they were. Ahead lay the final barrier to the Hellespont – an almost vertical wall of limestone, dotted with plenty of footholds. He was sure he could smell the sea. Thirty metres above, pinpricks of pale, milky light penetrated the darkness.

Moonlight! In the past I never gave the moon or stars a second thought but now they somehow feel important...

He checked his watch. "It's two in the morning. Dad'll be conked out in bed. Probably with his phone switched off."

"Indech is awake, Shay-An, looking, searching. Call your father on your device."

He flipped on the mobile. After a seemingly never-ending wait, the instrument bleeped gently, illuminating their lined faces in its eerie green glow. "It's working," he breathed.

He highlighted his father's number then hesitated. *So much depends on what happens when I press that very button. My life perhaps...*

He pushed and waited. After what seemed an eternity, the word *CALLING* scrolled across the screen.

"It works, Elatha, it works," he said, punching the air.

Another six seconds of nail biting followed before the word DAD appeared.

Then a ringing sound.

Chapter 21

In bright moonlight, Tubs and Zara leapt from the boat onto Granddad's small quay and hammered up the steps towards the cottage. As Mr Donnegan reached the garden gate, Zara was already balanced on Tubs' shoulders, scrutinising the carving above the doorway. A torch between her teeth, she fingered the edges of the interconnecting circles then switched her attention to the centre of the eye.

"Aha," she said, beaming the light on the central protuberance, no larger than a pea. She pressed it firmly. Nothing happened. "It's stuck. I need something to free it."

"Mr D," shouted Tubs. "Got a mallet or somethin'?"

Mr Donnegan dashed inside and returning with his toolbox, passed a hammer upwards.

"Get a move on, Zara. Your trainers are skinnin' my shoulders."

"Stop moaning," she said, tapping the copper nipple. "It still won't move; don't think I'm strong enough." She struck harder a second time and a dull chirr sounded. The centre of the eye slid slowly open, exposing the rectangular cavity behind. Her hand shot to her nose.

"What's up?" called Mr Donnegan.

"What a stink," she said. "This thing hasn't been opened in ages."

Carefully probing the interior with her fingers, she slowly extracted a handkerchief-sized square of soft leather. Then a pouch. Checking that nothing else lay inside, she closed the eye and leapt down.

"What about that?" she said triumphantly, handing the find to Mr Donnegan.

"What is it?" said Tubs.

"A map, Finbar, and a key – to one helluva big door, by the looks of it. Something's written on it: *S-c-a-e-n...*"

Zara punched the air. "We've a key to open the Scaen Gate! Wonder what's inside the purse?"

She loosened the thongs and shaking the contents free, four rough, identical coins fell out into Tubs' palm. He turned the pieces over. One side showed a crowned man's head; the reverse was blank except for a tri-circular design with a single eye at the centre. The word *FOMORI* was engraved at the base.

"Reckon they're worth much, Mr D?"

"They're gold, Finbar; definitely valuable."

"Forget the coins," Zara said. "Check if that map will help us find Shane."

Mr Donnegan unfolded the chart and turning it this way and that, began examining the crisscrossed lines of blues, reds, and greens. Realising the map was upside down, Tubs slid it from between Mr Donnegan's fingers and having turned it the right way up, handed it back.

"Er, thanks, Finbar. What do you make of it?"

Zara rolled her eyes. "Obviously it's some sort of chart of Clare Island."

"Were you expectin' a street map of New York?"

"Ha-bloody-ha," said Zara.

Embossed with a series of numbers and arrows pointing in different directions, the parchment depicted the island's main geographical features. In the top right hand corner, the four points of the compass were delineated in black and red ink.

Mr Donnegan was backcombing his hair with his fingers. "This thing is weird. The ancient Celts didn't use writing, as far as I know."

"Look, Mr D," said Tubs pointing, "the *Scaen gate* is right there. There's two other entry points with more odd-ball names – *Ilion* and *Scamander*. The coloured numbers on the side show at what depths those openin's are: green for low tide; red for high. Stands to reason." He looked up, a challenge in his eyes.

"Sounds plausible, Finbar. I suppose."

"Knowin' the tides and where those gates are, Mr D, means we can get inside to…"

"…What about those capital letters, Finbar: E, F, M, A and…?"

"…Mm," said Tubs, rubbing his forehead. "Days of the week…? No. Got it; they stand for the months of the year. Each number refers to the different tide markin's, so…."

"…Are we all on the same page, Finbar? E, F, M doesn't stand for any names on any calendar that *I* know…"

"It's in Irish, Mr D. E's for *Eanair*, January. B is for *Bealtaine*, May. Get it?"

Mr Donnegan nodded grudgingly. "Good man, Finbar, my Irish is real rusty. But how can we get inside if the gates are underwater? What about that one on land, the *Ilion*?"

"No chance," Zara said. "That one is half way up a cliff face. You'd need to be a seagull to get in. We'll have to get in by one of the other…"

A jarring buzz cut her short.

Mr Donnegan didn't look up from the map but muttered, "That's my mobile. I left it in the kitchen."

"I'll get it, Mr Donnegan."

Zara returned holding the phone at arm's length, as if it were an unexploded bomb.

"What is it, Zara?"

"It's Shane," she croaked. "Calling from some-where…"

"Shane," cried Mr Donnegan, grabbing the mobile. "Shane, where are you? Are you O.K.? Where…"

The voice at the other end crackled indistinctly.

"Listen, Dad, little time, phone doesn't work well here. Just lucky to………this call. Things are real bad here………I'm deep inside Clare Island ……Indech, the mad druid."

"Did you say *druid*, son?"

"Long story, no time to explain…"

"…Exactly where are you? Underground, you say?"

"Yes, deep underground caves but now we're as near to the surface of Clare Island as we can get. The mobile doesn't work so well so… I'm going to try and get out by one of the gates, tomorrow morning if I can…"

"…We've a map, so listen carefully, son. The most suitable gate for the tide is the Scaen…" He spread the map across his knees. "I'll be at the Gate at daybreak, without fail, in *Faith*…"

"…Yeah, but hurry …because... Have a girl helping me………be a problem."

"We have a key, Shane, so we'll either get in ourselves or you try to be as near as possible to that Gate. If not, we'll be outside, waiting. Did you get that? Sure you're OK?"

"I'm OK. And listen, I know about…Bres…"

"Fresh?"

"Bres the Fomorian …… and all ……………we'll be at that Gate from dawn. Phone us when you're close by…"

The line went dead.

Zara yanked Mr Donnegan's sleeve. "Did I hear some-thing about a girl?"

"It sounds bad. He was on about a druid or something."

"*Druid?*"

"An awful line. I must get a few things, excuse me."

He strode into his bedroom and slid a gun case down from the topmost shelf of the wardrobe. Chunky and heavy in its wool-lined container, the weapon was still spotless, glistening dully with protective oil to keep out the corrosive sea air. The magazine was still full of rounds, each bullet showing a tiny exposed lead tip. Sliding the dusty holster under his arm, he sighed and switched off the light.

"What have you got there, Mr D?"

"Dad's sidearm; he and Uncle Lionel were twin brothers; they served together in the Falklands War, 1982."

Tubs's tongue flicked over his lips. "A gun?"

"I hate these things, Finbar. They only cause trouble but once in a while they can help balance things. We must get back to the island."

"Don't you think this is gettin' very dodgy? Shouldn't we go to the police?"

"Waste of time. We must be at that Gate at dawn. Another problem is I don't know these seas at all. Making a night crossing is far too dangerous with those dodgy lights. Try and get some sleep. We'll head off first thing in the morning."

"Now I know why Shane's always seemed so different..." Tubs didn't complete the sentence as he brushed past and closed his bedroom door.

The moon was fading before anyone nodded off.

Chapter 22

Shane flicked off the phone, elated that his luck was finally changing for the better.

"Yessir, it worked," he said, smiling at Elatha. "Dad'll be at a place called the *Scaen* Gate at sunrise. Know it?"

"A healthy walk." She frowned. "But your father will need a special key to enter the island from the outside. Only Watchers carry them."

"Dad says he has one."

Her face puckered. "How could an Up-Worlder be in possession of a key? And no matter; the exits are always guarded."

"By who?"

"By whom," she corrected. "Watchers or Cyclopes."

Shane didn't want his disappointment to show. *If Elatha is right then my chances of getting out of here are close to zero. But there must be some other way; I'll think of something. I must.*

"Two of the entry zones lie beneath the sea surface," she continued.

"Isn't one situated on dry land?"

"Yes, but it's located on a steep cliff."

"Take me to the *Scaen*," he said brightly, trying to sound upbeat, determined to put a brave face on it at least.

"Sometimes we have problems opening the barriers. You need strength to operate them. I need rest, Shay-An."

"Let's get to the Gate first. Then we'll crash out 'til morning."

She grabbed his hand. "Come; to avoid the guards we must use a side pathway, not the main route."

Shane felt his spirits rise. The trip was downhill all the way – only rarely did he have to scramble on all fours or wiggle through perpendicular slits before they reached the dusty approaches to the gate. Using their elbows to inch forward, they reached the edge of the ridge that over-looked the Gate from a distant elevation.

The narrow gap between his head and the stone ceiling allowed him a panoramic view of the deserted clearing below. Straight ahead sloped the smooth exterior wall of the island. Wooden rafts and mounds of netting lay scattered around two upturned coracles. The floor was littered with discarded sea shells; rusting harpoons stood against the walls. In the shadows, a cobweb-covered boat lay on its side; its dragon-shaped prow splintered, its single mast fractured and jagged. Crumbling shields hung from its cracked timbers. Shane's attention switched to the three-metre square bulkhead that seemed to dominate everything.

Wow! The Scaen Gate is massive.

The gate was positioned between two identical wooden-spoked wheels, each the height of a man. Long handles projected from both rims. On nearby timber platforms sat a further series of gearwheels of ever-diminishing diameters, all joined by an arrangement of separate long axles. A complex progression of levers and pulleys were linked to the bronze entrance that was inserted into the wall of the island. Protruding from the framework, numerous lugs and spigots were fitted, all connected to the opening mechanism through a complexity of interlocking bars and chains.

"It needs two able-bodied people to work it, Shay-An," Elatha whispered.

"Then why do we need a key?"

"Before turning the wheels, you must open the main lock. The entrance always remains closed, otherwise the seas would flood everywhere."

"But it must stick out like a sore thumb from the outside."

"Our engineers have camouflaged it with special colourings. They have also painted images of seaweeds on the exterior surfaces."

"Let's give it a go now – there's nobody's about."

"Impossible. It is essential to know the level of the tides."

"Where do we get that info?"

"It is written in chalk on yonder darkboard."

"What are we waiting for?"

They backtracked on tiptoe through a low passageway to reach the deserted thoroughfare that led to the gate. Having spent so many hours without proper lighting, Shane found it hard to adjust to the glare of the adjacent wall torches as he read aloud the letters on the blackboard:

20 Iú [M]

LT 06.20

LM 12.35

After thinking for a few moments he ventured, "*LT* must stand for *low tide*, right?"

"So what does *LM* mean, Up-Worlder?"

"Mm, beats me."

"*20 Iú* is today, the twentieth of *Iúil*, July. M stands for *maidin* - morning. *LT* is *Lag Trá* or low tide, at twenty past six this morning when the gate can open. *LM* means the next *Lán Mara*, or high tide."

Shane beamed. "I was right then; *LT* does mean low tide."

"You were right by being wrong," she snapped.

Inclining an ear, he could hear the caress of water smoothly sweeping over metal. *So near, yet so far away.* He pointed. "That wrecked ship's full of spiders. What's all that about?"

"Nothing was safe from those Viking warships. They butchered everything along the West Coast but they attacked Clare Island only once. Their pirate fleet only expected helpless farmers, not armed Cyclopes. Only two of their craft escaped. That long ship is a relic of that bygone time."

Shane checked his watch. "Roll on the morning. We'll do two-hour shifts apiece, I'll take the first watch." *She looks all in; I'll do the whole night watch, she deserves a decent sleep.* "Worried about your folks, Elatha?"

She nodded.

"I'm sure they'll be OK," he said with a cheerfulness he didn't remotely feel. He positioned one of the gourds into a makeshift pillow. "No mattresses and duvets around here, eh?"

"You get used to sleeping in the open. At least it's never cold."

Taking one of the daggers from his belt he placed it across his knee and yawned loudly.

Hearing the slight cracking noise his jaws made, she lightly rubbed his face. "Good night, Shay-An."

"Night, Elatha."

In the ensuing silence, he was aware of the thudding in his eardrums as she sighed, rested her head and arm across his chest and instantly fell asleep.

Chapter 23

Mr Donnegan switched off the incessant alarm. The grey light told him the morning was wet and miserable; the last thing he wanted. He made his way into the hallway and trying to sound cheerful, hollered, "Rise and shine." Getting no response, he peeped into Zara's room. It was empty and her bed made.

"I've been up for ages, Mr Donnegan," came her call from the kitchen.

He knocked on the second bedroom and entered. Still submerged under the bedcovers, Tubs' attention was on the weather.

"Seen outside, Mr D? It's biblical out there."

Mr Donnegan opened the curtains. Under normal circumstances, he would have had second thoughts about taking a boat out in such conditions. But these were far from normal conditions.

"Up and at 'em, Finbar. We're ready to go."

"What about brekker?"

"Prepared everything last night; ham and pickle sandwiches and coffee. We'll eat on the way."

In the dismal dawn, Clare Island loomed forebodingly on the horizon. The wind was brisk and white horses were rising as *Faith* butted her way out of the estuary and into the open Atlantic. Tubs retched regularly over the side. By 6.05 they had turned across the southern side of the island and into a freshening gale.

Mr Donnegan put down his binoculars and closed the *Pocket Tide Guide.* "The *Scaen Gate* is covered by the tide," he said, unable to hide his disappointment. "Zara, check the map for the next nearest Gate and…"

"…I've already checked. The Scamander Gate is also underwater."

Throttling back the engine, Mr Donnegan swung the wheel and pointed *Faith's* nose towards the harbour. "You take her in, Finbar," he muttered, his voice low. He slumped into the pilot's chair, buried his face in his hands and added, "We can't do a thing to save my son."

His face almost the colour of his green oilskins, Tubs said, "Sorry, Mr D, but I'm not great at steerin' boats…"

"…You fluff ball," snorted Zara, pushing Tubs aside and taking the wheel. "I'll lock us on to a course for the island."

Three minutes later, she realised Mr Donnegan hadn't moved and was still staring at his feet. She locked the wheel and said, "Mr Donnegan, give me your mobile. Too much wind up here to make a call; I'm going below. Tubs, just keep an eye on things, right?"

Without raising his eyes, Mr Donnegan dejectedly handed over his phone and in two strides Zara was inside *Faith's* claustrophobic cabin, trying to retain her balance against the rocking of the boat. Finally she steadied herself sufficiently to locate then press Shane's number. For eight eternal seconds she stood with the phone held to her ear, trying to block out the sounds of the wind and the irritating coke can rolling back and forth across the deck above. The sudden *buzz buzz* of a call being connected made her punch the air and shout, "YES!"

***

Shane shook Elatha awake and pointed. "Someone's down there," he mouthed.

It was 6.18.

They scampered from their sleeping place towards the vantage slot overlooking the Gate. In the strange glow – a mixture of torchlight combining with lights from some

144

other hidden source – they inched forwards. Ten metres below, an overweight young man was rising to his feet from a makeshift bed, yawning and stretching. Rubbing his eyes, he pulled a package of food from a shoulder bag.

"That's Forgal," hissed Elatha. "A trainee Watcher."

"By himself by the looks of things."

What best to do? Risk everything, rush Forgal, wrench open the doors and take my chances in the water? A clatter sounding in the distance made him stiffen then slowly sink to his knees and out of sight. *Marching feet. Trouble.* Round the nearest bend, some fifty metres to his right, strode Indech, golden scepter in hand. Four armed men marched two by two behind. As they paraded forwards, Shane saw Forgal leap to attention.

"Have you had a quiet guard?" Indech asked conversationally. He looked anything but friendly.

"Not a thing st… stirring, sir."

Like a hungry shark, the druid's sweeping gaze took in everything then refocused on Forgal. "You've been on guard the whole night, yes?"

"Or course, sir. I was just, er, having some breakfast."

Shane blinked, finding it hard to believe that someone had been sleeping such a short distance from where he and Elatha had spent the night.

Without warning Indech grabbed Forgal by the throat. "Shane Dunne has badly injured Manderas and Lugh. Elatha helped the Up-World savage escape the pool. I will personally see to it that she pays for her actions. You be sure to keep your eyes and ears open, otherwise…"

At that moment, the local telecommunications mast checked the last known location of Shane's mobile, fed the information to its central computer and Zara's call was transferred to a position eight and a half kilometres off the Mayo coastline. Above and behind Indech's men, the rock'n'roll ringtone of Shane's mobile shattered the morning silence like an explosion. The incessant tune, magnified by the hollow cave, resonated and echoed, exposing Shane's hiding place with appalling clarity.

Shane backed away, fumbling and groping as he tried to wrench the mobile from his jeans. Ten bars of the melody had sounded before he succeeded in switching it off.

"What was *that*?" gasped Elatha, her eyes unnaturally wide.

"I forgot to switch the mobile to silent."

"Up there," came Indech's shout as he ushered his men left and right. He pointed to Shane's hiding place. "I want them alive."

As one, Shane and Elatha scrambled backwards before sliding down the short incline, almost out of control. Hitting the ground first, Shane flipped on the torch.

"We've a thirty second head start," he panted. "Not a moment more."

"The map. We must decide which direction to take."

She's right. If we stop at intervals to check the map, instead of running blind, we'll make faster progress.

Commanding himself to ignore the whistles of Indech's men being answered by more distant calls, he unfolded the map under torchlight. It only took five seconds for Elatha to decide and they were off again, full pace into the semi-darkness, their clothes already damp with sweat.

There. A tall shaft of light ahead. Maybe an exit?

Shane bounded towards the cleft and scanned the deserted track below. The shouts and pounding feet behind hastened his decision. Leaping into the open and with Elatha close behind, he sprinted across and thundered down the stairway. He didn't need a map to tell him where it led – downward towards the volcano.

"Fast as we can, Elatha; we're younger and faster. We can outrun them. Let's go."

Indech, coming around the corner, smirked as he glimpsed the flowing blonde hair dropping from view.

Chapter 24

No matter how fast they ran, the sound of following footsteps and angry frustrated voices were never far behind. After a punishing thirty minutes, Shane stopped to unfold the map with trembling hands.

"I cannot hear any footsteps," wheezed Elatha, "Maybe we have lost them?"

"I don't trust Indech, he's up to something. Maybe he's told his men to follow us in silence? Let's just keep going at full lick; push as hard as we possibly can to where these paths cross ..." He tapped the map. "...Say for five minutes? Can you do it?"

She nodded.

He smiled wanly and stroked her face. "Remember, flat out," he said, handing her the map.

The pathway was flat and well-trodden making their progress easier but no less exhausting. Where the two passageways crossed, they stopped, lungs heaving, hands on their knees, sodden with sweat.

"That was seriously fast, Elatha," he panted. "We're almost there."

They helter-skeltered downwards in blind confusion along the steep incline until Shane raised an arm. Bumping heavily into each other, they careered to an eventual standstill. Above the sound of their rasping breaths, he heard a noise; footfalls sounding somewhere on the passageway above! And someone humming loudly.

A voice called, "Prepare yourselves for the infliction of pain."

Indech! He has us trapped like rats.

He swallowed his fear, grabbed Elatha's hand and tore off down the remaining three flights of stairs, desperation lending extra speed to his legs. They almost toppled down the last section, knees and hips trembling, heads ringing with fatigue.

Coming to a halt, Shane wheezed, "We're trapped. Gimme the map again."

He whipped it from Elatha's hand and jammed it beneath the torchlight. "Look; where the rubbish chute drops into the volcano at the end of this passage. We've a chance; there's another way out; it's marked; small print; '*The Catacombs*'."

"I've never entered that section before…"

"…It's our only hope. Come on."

They raced towards what appeared to be a dead end, and dead end it was – a perpendicular barrier of solid rock. Shane frantically checked the surface for a possible means of escape. There was none. The heat was making matters worse and he could feel the irritation in his lungs increasing in the gas-laden atmosphere. More in desperation than in hope, he scrutinised the wall's uppermost layer.

"There," he breathed.

Four metres above ground, where the wall and the roof of the passageway met, lay a long horizontal breach in the rock face. Concealed in shadow, it was barely wide enough for a body to squeeze through.

Shane interlocked the fingers of both hands, forming a makeshift stirrup. Elatha then placed a foot into his cupped palms and in the same movement, he launched her powerfully towards the ledge. She grabbed hold of the lip and hoisting herself upwards, scrambled into the opening. Seconds later her head peeped over the ledge.

"There is sufficient room for two," she gasped, "but hurry."

He took a flying leap at the wall and began clawing his way up the irregular surface. He managed to find some lucky hand and footholds as he clambered upwards until Elatha was able to grasp his shoulders and drag him in. Hearts pumping, they retreated on their stomachs into the cramped hollow, flattened themselves against the ground and waited.

Indech soon appeared, whistling tunelessly, convinced the pair were finally cornered. Behind, sauntered four armed guards and two Cyclopes. Finding nobody on his arrival, the druid's walking pace changed and he ran forwards and peered over the ledge leading to the volcano.

"Dead end, sir," the leading soldier called. "Maybe they've found a hole somewhere and...?"

"...I will find them, you imbecile. Bring me the Locator-Max."

A soldier ran forward carrying a small wooden box. From it he removed and unwrapped a crystal cube, no bigger than a half-sized football, and placed it on an adjacent slab. Indech cupped the black object, staring into its interior, his hands slowly moving this way and that as if trying to wipe away invisible smoke or unseen film clinging to the glassy surface. His sinuous fingers spread and stretched as he bent closer, intent, lips in a straight line. Behind, the silent guards shuffled uneasily.

After a few moments Indech replaced the artefact then straightened. Shane stopped breathing as the druid pointed unerringly to where he and Elatha lay face downward in the shadows.

"The Up-Worlder and the vixen have escaped into the Catacombs," he said, his voice soft and neutral.

"Shall we follow them, sir?"

"No, hungry bellies will have them out sooner or later. Post guards at each exit. I have more pressing matters to attend to."

Without warning, Indech lurched forward and almost fell.

"Are you alright, sir?"

"I'm perfectly alright. Just a little lightheaded. Water, quickly. That antique relic; it can tell much but…" He sat on a nearby rock. "A few seconds to recover then we march on."

***

Shane didn't speak until the sound of footsteps had long faded. "What was Indech staring into?"

"The Locator-Max, one of the kingdom's most prized treasures. The device can detect missing people or those who get lost in our deepest caves. It can locate most things although it can sap much of the user's energy in some strange way. In olden times many died trying to explore its properties. It can also…"

"…So *that's* how Indech has always been one step ahead; he knows where everyone is. Where are we now?"

Before answering, she removed a short stick from her bag and jammed a compact bung of black tar on the end. She extracted two white stones from her tunic and once, twice, three times struck them against each other, sending a succession of sparks into the air. Leaning over, she blew through her cupped hands, inducing the flames to spread into the wad. Shane took a small backward step to avoid the darts of yellow flames flicking upwards, realising just how gaunt their faces were.

She looked again over her shoulder. "Our parents never failed to threaten feeding us to the Catacomb monsters if we didn't eat our seaweed. Lugh explored here once, bailing out twine behind him as he descended, otherwise he would have perished in the endless maze of tunnels. Something happened to him down here. He refused to speak about it."

Shane pointed at the map. "What's this *Terra Incognita*?" He watched her head shake in irritation. *I notice she always gets a bit narky when she doesn't know the answer to something...* "Also somebody's signature; *Beoan, son of Mellan;* a mate of Indech's?"

"Beoan was our mapmaker."

"Maybe he didn't want Indech to know about this place? What's that wiggly line at the bottom; looks like a snake; what does it mean?"

"I do not know. Let us move from here."

Shane stared as the torch threw demonic shapes around the defile. *These caves feel different from the rest of the Kingdom.* Whereas his feet felt less liable to roll and twist, the place was clammier, making him want to glance over his shoulder. The track increased in width, winding through a succession of caverns and high-ceilinged tunnels. To the left and right, dim subways and underpasses led off at irregular intervals, suggesting the trails had previously been used but not for some considerable time.

Shane stopped. "I could eat my arm off."

"Oh, no!" she cried, turning her bag upside down. "Only the goorama remains; the rest must have fallen out when escaping from Indech."

"We'll ration what we have. What's goorama anyway?"

"Mashed fish eggs mixed with shark oil and cliff spinach."

He shuddered, remembering that his all-time hate was spinach – followed closely by fish eggs.

"Rank," he said under his breath, watching her divide the dark cake. His nose twitched.

"What troubles you, Shay-An?"

"Funny smell."

"It is smoke from the volcano."

"No, we're moving away from the heat. Fishy smell…"

"Perhaps mother's cooking affects your nose? Eat."

Despite his reservations, the goorama was delicious. He glanced around again, still unable to shake off the uncomfortable eeriness of their new surroundings.

***

After another long bout of marching, he felt the increase in temperature. Also, his footfalls were no longer producing echoes; nor were any rock formations visible. He sensed rather than saw the boundless opening ahead. It wasn't a nice feeling, as the light no longer showed anything, just vast empty nothingness. Keeping the torch extended with his right hand, he led Elatha with his left, slowly inching forward, feeling rather than seeing the rim of the abyss ahead. He stopped. A sheer drop fell away into a blackness so profound that it seemed to pull his eyesight down into it, making them both feel giddy. Shane repeatedly swept his torch across the gorge but could discern little of the far side except dark, irregular shapes.

"It is truly deep," came Elatha's hushed voice.

Shane kicked a stone over the edge. His ear cocked to the abyss, he listened, waiting to hear a distant clatter but no sound came. Even after a count of thirty. "You'd probably die from old age before you hit the bottom."

"Perhaps it leads to the centre of the world, Shay-An?"

"I'm going to scout for a way over. Light me another of your torches. You wait here. I won't be long."

I know she hates being left on her own but I don't want to risk both our lives at the same time.

Three minutes later, his shout made her jump. "Over here."

He was standing some three hundred metres away, at the foot of a narrow footbridge that curved across the canyon. Using the torch, he could just about make out where the stone arc joined with the far side. The primitive bridge was ancient, its dilapidated state suggesting it hadn't been crossed for a very long time.

"It must lead somewhere, Elatha. Anyway, I've checked; there's no other way across."

"Is it sufficiently sturdy?"

The same question's been bugging me; it has no handrail; one slip means certain death.

Chapter 25

"Only one way to find out," Shane said, trying to sound optimistic. Placing his right foot on the bridge, he tested it against his weight before sliding the left forward. "Seems solid enough," he said, signalling Elatha to follow.

Best not tell her I've no head for heights; even the funfair rollercoaster used to make me feel yukky.

He wiped his palms against his jeans and lightheaded, moved forward, gingerly placing one foot down before taking a further step.

"Hold the back of my belt with one hand," he said, "and try not to look down."

I don't even want to think about how far it is to the bottom. Could it really lead to the Earth's centre?

He stopped as a small stone lodged beneath the sole of his trainer. Rather than flick it aside, he slowly lifted his weight and carefully, very carefully, rolled the pebble away, until he knew it had toppled into the abyss. He didn't bother waiting to hear if it struck bottom.

"Why have you stopped, Shay-An?" croaked Elatha.

"Didn't want you to trip on a stone."

He edged onwards, focusing only on the far side, continuing to shuffle rather than walk. Their progress was horribly slow, with neither daring to stare into the unfathomable blackness cloying at their feet. Shane shone his torch into the abyss below, then into the almost solid darkness above; each were equally impenetrable. This completed the feeling of his being virtually alone in a world of funereal nothingness. Eventually realising that one false move by either meant certain death to them both, Elatha released her grip on Shane's belt. After two further minutes of eternity, Shane's clothes were stuck to his skin. Suddenly he felt the gradient change as the bridge began to slope gently downwards. Instinctively he increased his forward rate until Elatha whispered, "Slower, Shay-An, *please.*"

His nerves were so taut he hadn't fully grasped what she'd said but he understood the warning by her terrified tone. "Sorry," he mumbled.

Plagued by fearful lightheadedness but knowing that the far side of the chasm just had to be getting closer, Shane lengthened his step. He felt Elatha's fingers bite into his back. "No, Shay-An, slower."

For their remaining time on the bridge, neither dared speak nor communicate with each other until Shane gasped, "Wow," and leapt onto land. Supporting Elatha's weight as she took the final step to safety, he added, "I'm whacked out. Let's grab a little rest."

Elatha blew her cheeks out and sat down on the nearest boulder. "I am fatigued also."

They heard a new sound, a regular drip-drip echoing nearby. And then a faster trickle, followed by the welcome sound of rushing water percolating through rock. Shane went off to find the stream, gourds in hand. He returned quickly.

"Lovely fresh stuff. Ours was getting warm and stale."

They drank the teeth-achingly fresh water and swallowed what remained of the goorama before stretching out on the floor. Perhaps it was the exhaustion combined with the relief of the safe crossing, but within minutes, both were asleep.

The smell woke Shane. The same one as before.

He lay on his back, half dreaming it was rise'n'shine, with the aroma of breakfast wafting from the kitchen. Bacon, eggs, fried bread and Aunt Agnes' sweet, sweet tea. With a sense of crushing disappointment, he remembered where he was. Elatha's torch was out. Then came the sound.

Nearby, a large bulk was moving. No, it was sliding, or to be more precise, slithering. He remained immobile, senses keyed. He heard it again. There could be no doubt; something was making its way towards them along a nearby gradient.

Somebody pulling something? Can't be. That seafood pong. Fish? Up here?

He carefully slid the flashlight into his palm. With his other hand he inched one of Lugh's daggers free. *Why am I holding this weapon? – I hate knives. This is the first time in my life I ever felt like I might have to use one...*

All around everything was composed of immobile black shapes. He could feel Elatha move in her sleep as he very slowly turned his head towards the bizarre sounds. As the flashlight came on, he froze. Elatha's head was resting close to a circular aperture in the rock, and there, no more than half a metre away, was the most gigantic eel he had ever seen. Its head was larger than a man's. Cold eyes that had been riveted on Elatha's throat were now dazzled by sudden light and the fang-filled jaws involuntarily closed, then reopened in surprise. It hissed viciously, blinking in the light.

Shane reacted instinctively by ramming the torch into its face. At the same time he struck with the knife handle, bringing it down in a vicious arc, making contact above the creature's left eye. Instead of encountering soft tissue, he felt the butt of the weapon jar painfully against cartilage. As the serpent hissed and jerked away, Shane toppled sideways, sending his dagger across the cave floor. Cobra-like, the eel darted and spat as it attacked the still revolving knife. Shane bellowed and lunged, flinging his water gourd into the eel's face. Razor sharp teeth sank into the swollen bag, which burst open, splattering its contents over the serpent's head and neck. Puzzled and angry, it glared malevolently before slithering backwards along the shaft, at a speed remarkable for a beast of its size. Although the whole incident had only taken a few seconds, Elatha was already upright, her hand grasping her throat.

"What... what was that?" she said, her voice hoarse, her face a mask of horror.

Shane picked up the weapon and replaced it in his belt. "Some sort of monstrous eel. Another couple of seconds and it would've ripped your head off. About ten metres long. It had small claws all the way along its body."

"We have been most fortunate."

"I know that but...?"

"...What you saw was a giant eel; we rear them to provide us with electricity."

"I never want to see or smell fish again. Let's get away from this godawful place."

"Any attack is usually fatal. They hunt in packs; there may be others close by. Quickly."

Chapter 26

Inside *Faith's* cabin, Zara continued to hold the mobile at arm's length, listening as the message repeated: *"The caller has either hung up or the number you have dialled is currently unavailable. Please try again later."* She switched it off and scrambled back on deck. Overhead, the cries of the gulls were harsh and piercing in the crisp air.

Tubs began gnawing his fingertips as her haggard face came into view. "Did you get through, Zara?"

"The thing rang and then for some reason cut off. Just like that. Weird."

Tubs blurted, "Didn't you try again?"

Zara speared him with one of her looks. "The line went dead; D – E – A – D, understand?"

Mr Donnegan stood up with difficulty, took back his phone and stared sightlessly into the distance. "It's bad enough," he said, his voice small and weak, "knowing Shane's so close. I feel so damned helpless. Just as well his mother isn't here; she wouldn't be able to handle this…"

Zara noted Mr Donnegan had perked up a little although he still looked floored. She hated it when adults got all gloomy and morose – it's no use complaining when things don't go your way, you have to try and change them.

"Maybe his battery was runnin' low, Mr D?"

"Do you want me to take her into the island, Mr Donnegan?"

"I'll do it, Zara," he replied, wearily retaking the wheel.

The harbour was already astir but the ever-present marine stink of oil was now dampened by the wind and rain. The engines of the Achill Island lifeboat were ticking over and three small search craft were already moving out into the swell. A subdued crowd stood on the pier, many blowing on cupped hands or stretching their limbs to keep warm. On the esplanade, a yawning Sergeant Canny was buttoning up his uniform.

"More bad news, I'm afraid, sir," he called, grabbing the mooring rope and easing *Faith* against the jetty.

Mr Donnegan tried to keep the frustration from his voice. "*Bad* news, you say?"

If the policeman heard the sarcasm he ignored it. "Minister Roache is callin' the whole thing off, sayin' it's a waste of taxpayers' money, like. Them civil servants up in Dublin reckon your boy's either lost at sea or, well you know, sharks…"

"…It sounds to me," interrupted Zara, hands on her hips, "that the Minister is more concerned with saving pennies than lives."

"It's nuttin' to do with me, missy, orders, but I'll be havin' to stand down the search by late evenin'. We'll still be keepin' a weather eye out for young Shane, y'understand."

Mr Donnegan climbed ashore with difficulty. "I bet if the bloody Minister's own son was missing they'd be out every hour of the day and night." His voice sounding weary, he added, "It's not your fault, sergeant, you did all you could."

"Tell you what, sir; I'll ask Captain O'Malley to use the ferry – him and me, unofficial, like – to scout around in the early mornin' and evenin' – see if we might locate that lad of yours."

"That's nice of you, sergeant, I appreciate…"

"…Join us if you feel like it, sir; and you too, missy. The *Island Queen* will cover more water in less time than that little skip of yours."

"Thanks, sergeant, that's great."

"Yeah, thanks, sarge," added Zara.

***

Such was their determination to put as much distance as possible between themselves and the electric eel, that Shane and Elatha moved at maximum pace wherever possible, pushing their bodies to the limit. After two hours of hard pacing and climbing, Shane, in the lead, stopped.

"I badly need a drink," he gasped. "Any of that goorama left?"

"I thought you didn't like fish eggs, Shay-An? Little remains; perhaps we should conserve it for later?"

"I could guzzle a bucket of ice cream but guess what I really fancy?" He rested the back of his head against an overhang. "I'd like to pig out on a giant pizza with all the trimmings, then murder a McDonalds."

"Murder Mac who?"

Shane chuckled. "McDonald is not really a person, it's a place where you go for hamburgers and…"

What had begun as a normal conversation, ended without the slightest warning. Shane felt himself grabbed abruptly from behind by muscular arms and effortlessly hoisted off the ground, despite his kicking and wriggling. It was a waste of time trying to break free; the restraining holds were massively strong as a blindfold was pulled over his head and ropes whipped around his limbs. Trussed and helpless, he knew he had been thrown over a massive shoulder and was being carried like a sack of potatoes for what seemed half a lifetime. Then came the smell of cooking fires and the sound of deep voices.

"Who are they, Malinmog?"

"I not know, Polydemos."

Cyclopes!

Shane fought against the crushing disappointment of this latest letdown – just his luck to be caught by some freelancing band of Indech's bounty hunters...*But wait.*

There was something very different about these Cyclopes. True, he and Elatha had been taken against their will but they'd been bound and gagged in an almost gentle manner. His captors lacked the naked aggression of Indech's lot; their voices were softer, devoid of overt spite and hate. He knew he was propped against a wall, resting on something warm and soft. What a change; he'd only felt one hundred percent hard stone under his body for as far back as he could remember.

"These are very young," came another shout.

"How did they get here?" A woman's incredulous voice.

"Why treat guests like animals?" boomed the authoritative voice of somebody new arriving.

"These must be Indech's spies, Homer. I've bound and gagged them. We cannot risk..."

"...Polydemos, we are not barbarians. Remove the folds. How often must I tell you that one is innocent until found to be otherwise?"

Shane blinked as the folds were removed. They were pinioned in a low-ceilinged and smoke-filled enclosure. A great fire burned in the spacious hearth, over which two cauldrons simmered. One wall was lined by sealskin boots with untidy piles of clothes stacked alongside. A table surrounded by many chairs occupied the middle of the room, reminding Shane of a Brisbane community centre. Five Cyclopes sat at the table, four men and a woman. Fur-covered packages lay scattered around and a sweaty smell pervaded. Ears erect, a massive, black hound stood close by, the largest dog Shane had ever seen.

These people are nothing like Indech's grumpy Cyclopes.

With a shock he saw that many were albinos, their skins an off-white colour, hair similarly so. Their hands were smooth.

"My name is Homer," began the bearded Cyclops with the opaque, featureless eye. "I am often called the Bard. Forgive the ropes and blindfolds but we fear, with great justification, all intruders from above."

"And from below," said somebody else.

Homer paused before asking, "Are you allied with Indech?"

Shane paused. *Are these people friends or accomplices of the mad druid? Should I fudge my answer and try and bide my time? Our lives may depend on what I say...*

Homer sensed Shane's hesitation. "Always speak the truth, young man. Although I am now blind − our eyesight suffers greatly from having no sunlight – I can tell whether someone spouts lies or not... from the tiny tremors in the voice. Your speech identifies you as an Up-Worlder. Fear not, we will treat you fairly, regardless of your utterances."

"My name is Shane and I'm no friend of Indech. Neither is Elatha."

"I hear only frankness and honesty. Malinmog, free them. Penelope, these people are our guests. Bring forth food and drink. Now, inform us of who you are and what brings you here, so far underground."

After the introductions were completed, two soup bowls were placed on the table. Homer signalled Shane and Elatha to sit.

"Your innards must sing with hunger. We receive few travellers at this time of year."

A polite wave of laughter rippled through the group. In spite of their recent travails and the strangeness of their surroundings, Shane grinned at Elatha.

"What's this food called?" he asked brightly, determined to get off on the right foot. "Really good," he added, turning to Elatha for confirmation as they both tucked in.

"It's sea louse," said Homer.

"A louse?" hooted Shane, almost dropping his spoon.

Homer smiled. "Not like the creature you know in the Up-World, the woodlouse. Ours is half the length of a man's arm. It lives around the geysers welling from the sea floor. Its flesh resembles lobster, no?"

Never having tasted lobster, Shane nonetheless nodded.

"My real name is Sarpaedion but I am universally addressed as Homer."

"Why's that, er, Homer?"

"I have held the position of Master Poet for many years and I currently train a few apprentices. Penelope, dear, place your hands on them. Be not alarmed, strangers, my wife can read one's aura; a facility handed down to us by the Tuatha de Dannan. She will identify your origins. Today, such skills are retained by only a special few."

Out of the corner of his mouth Shane whispered, "What's an aura, Elatha?"

"Everyone has an energy halo surrounding their body..."

"...Like a saint's halo?"

"A special glow that radiates from every human..."

"...You mean a person's soul?"

Penelope's approach ended their exchange. Her bulk stretched above them, as she held her gnarled hands a little above their heads. Shane stared at her wrinkled face, trying to fathom her age. *Seriously old.* Staring fixedly at some spot on his forehead, she swept her hands back and forth, never more than a few centimetres above his hair, grazing his ears and nose.

Straightening up, she called, "Both are Fomorian; he a recent arrival."

"An Up-Worlder cannot enter our kingdom," said Homer sharply. "Perhaps, my dear, your recent illness has affected your abilities?" He addressed Shane. "Young man?"

"Well, it's a long story, Homer."

"Here in Lower Fomoria, we have little entertainment, so we rely greatly on our stories. Sometimes, yes, if I'm strong enough, I recite the Fomorian Odyssey, which takes long hours. Once this great story was the highlight of our feast days and festivals. Now its recounting has become a rarity. Malinmog, summon all. Shane will tell us his story."

Homer stepped down and aided by Penelope, vacated his tall, throne-like chair. Considerably older and different from all other chairs and benches in the room, Shane marvelled at its thick wooden legs and arms, each carved and inlaid with motifs of seabirds, waves and stars.

Malinmog placed a sealskin cushion on the chair and moved it closer to the fire. "The Seat of the Storyteller is yours," he announced.

Slightly flushed, Shane rose and deciding he'd rather stand, faced the overcrowded room.

Chapter 27

When he had finished, everyone in the audience applauded and not, Shane felt, just out of politeness. Nobody had spoken during his talk or interrupted. He'd skipped mentioning what had happened in the House of Hades because he was still too confused about it all.

"So," said Homer, "you are an enemy of Indech, as am I."

"But," said Shane, "I thought Indech was your leader?"

"Until he decreed that Cyclopes were '*to concentrate solely on work that required more of the body than of the mind*'. Despite working as a team of horses under the same chariot yoke throughout our history, we were overnight decreed second class citizens. I publicly declared no civilised Fomorian should accept Indech's barbaric changes and so began our rebellion."

"What happened?"

"Indech killed our leading Cyclopes and attempted to have me tried. Being tutor to King Tethra's family, I enjoyed royal protection, I was lucky to escape to live here in the Catacombs with my supporters, aided by friends above. A difficult existence."

Elatha spoke. "My parents helped you escape during the uprising."

"Indeed, we only broke out of jail because your mother hid a cell-door key inside a goorama cake."

"Tell me about those giant electric eels, Homer."

Homer stroked his beard. "We call them *eascann*. Their teeth snap fishing lines like a sliver of thread and they convert heat from the volcano into electricity to kill their prey. Sometimes they become stranded in the tunnels and in exchange for helping them by applying a little oil, they guard our gates. Their spear-sharp sense of smell allows them to locate intruders. They relish human flesh. We rejoice that they failed with you and Elatha."

"Yeah, right," muttered Shane.

"We are further protected by our giant snapping turtles, extinct in the Up-World. They are well trained to sever a leg without warning; another reason why Indech rarely ventures down here."

These Cyclopes speak in the same tone, never raising their voices whether they're chirpy or narky. "But how can Cyclopes, er, exist, here, in the twenty-first century?"

Homer pointed Shane towards the high, wooden throne. "Please sit in the Seat of the History and you will learn. Close your eyes, grasp the arms firmly and soon you will see, not hear, what took place. Long before men started to write, twin boys were born on our island with an appalling affliction, each had only one eye, in the middle of their foreheads..."

This Seat is moving underneath me. What's happening? I'm floating above the earth, as if ...I'm in the clouds, drifting above a pine forest. Snow falling. I'm shivering. Am I watching some weird historical film or am I taking part in some crazy computer game...?

"Look at our history..." whispered Homer, placing a reassuring hand on Shane's shoulder.

Shane watched as two huddled Cyclopean babies materialised out of the snow, lying on a blanket, crying...

Homer's voice broke through. "Our ancient laws decreed that all deformed newborns be killed - the twins you see have been abandoned to die..."

Shane held his breath as a bear approached the babes, hungrily surveying the unexpected meal in its path. The wailing stopped and two pairs of tiny hands shot upwards to fondle the fur of the female bear's breast. Puzzled, she remained motionless, staring downwards, nose twitching. Suddenly she bent and grasping the blanket in her teeth, slouched off towards her lair, a new family dangling from her jaws.

The scene faded to be replaced by a panorama of rugged, sun-drenched mountains. Mesmerised at what was taking place, Shane watched a well-dressed horseman riding through woodland then coming to a sudden halt. Arrows protruding from its abdomen, a dead bear lay in his path. Two one-eyed children sat on each side of the body, weeping inconsolably, calling for their "mother". Realising that local hunters had killed the bear, the elderly rider grasped the boys by the hand and led the orphans towards a sprawling homestead in the distance. As the scene faded into nothingness, Shane could hear the laughter of the young Cyclopes, growing to manhood in the safety of their rich, new environment.

"But, Homer, what happened to them?" blurted Shane, involuntarily opening his eyes and standing up.

In almost the same movement, Elatha pushed him back into the Seat. "Stop interrupting, Shay-An."

"Patience," added Homer, "just watch. Becoming formidable fighters, they were accepted back into the island community and when they married, their children inherited their fathers' abnormality. Nonetheless they thrived and generations later, all islanders had been replaced by this one-eyed race, the Cyclopes."

"But, Homer, why come here?"

Homer sighed. "Please watch; without interruption."

Shane was shocked into silence as a scene of catastrophic wreckage and destruction met his wide eyes. Both the islands of Thera and Cyclops lay in ruins. Fires blazed; buildings smouldered; bodies lay strewn on streets smashed and broken beyond repair. Thick, volcanic ash descended like heavy snow from thunderous skies. Spellbound, he watched as a small flotilla of ships, under oar and sail, were evacuating survivors from Thera. Simultaneously, a large boat, overladen with one-eyed men, women and children, was vacating Cyclops Island to join the Therians in a single convoy, all desperately heading to safety.

Shane spoke without opening his eyes. "Where are they going, Homer?"

Elatha grimaced. "Can you not keep quiet for a single moment?"

"Sorry, Elatha but this is like watching an exciting disaster movie."

Homer was shaking his head. "You are so impatient." He took a sip from his goblet. "After many wanderings the convoy arrived at Clare Island. Because our ships appeared without warning from half-submerged caves, the Christian monks later recorded us as being *one-eyed, undersea monsters*." Despite Homer's voice having remained calm throughout, he brought his fist down hard on the table. "Nowhere is it written that Ireland's music, dance and sports began with us, the Fomorians. You have had enough history for one day, eh?"

"Everyone would love history if we had that Seat back in St Columbanus," said Shane. "What about this Fomorian Mission I keep hearing about?"

172

Chapter 28

Homer didn't immediately respond.

"We Fomorians," he began, as if he'd made his mind up about something, "have long respected the sea. So, we set ourselves a Mission – to respect the things that coexist with us and to appreciate the creatures that provide us with food and enhance our lives with their presence. We only kill what we need; replant what we cut down; regrow what we harvest and waste nothing. Because of the Tuatha de Dannan, our Mission almost died. Today it is restricted to the seas."

Shane frowned. "Like how?"

"Most large swimming creatures in the world's oceans – whales, dolphin, shark have been killed. Massive trawlers, trailing nets that stretch great distances, catch millions of fish daily; undersized or unwanted catches are thrown to the gulls or converted into fertiliser. The seas around us are becoming underwater deserts."

"But what's that got to do with the Mission?"

"The Catacomb Cyclopes are still part of conserving what remains. Ah, there's Gargoylemog, he can explain these matters far better than I can."

A small, squat Cyclops dressed in green oilskins and a full-length rubber apron, appeared from a side entrance. The same height as Shane, and not much older, a large monocle and a whistle hung from his neck. At his heel strode a huge dog. He made no attempt to conceal his exasperation.

"You well know it's feeding time, Homer."

Homer reached out to locate then hold the young Cyclops' arm. "Shane, meet Gargoylemog, he is the hub of our Mission. He knows more about fish than anybody else alive."

Gargoylemog nodded, as if acknowledging that Homer was simply stating the obvious. "If you are quite done..."

"…. Perhaps you might show Shane around our Mission?"

Gargoylemog winced then lisped through the large gap in his front teeth. "Come, stay with me."

"Here, boy," said Shane, reaching out ruffling the hound's thick fur.

"Don't; he'll eat you; he'll…," screamed Gargoylemog, his palm across his nose and mouth. Seeing the animal licking Shane's hand he'd stopped mid-sentence.

Holding the dog's massive head in his hands, Shane looked up. "What's the hassle, Gargoylemog?"

The young Cyclops' eye was wide. "Argus answers only to Homer and me. He is trained to attack and kill. No one dares approach him. He has killed many of Indech's men."

Shane took a quick backward step but the dog followed, nuzzling his jeans. "Good, er, boy," he mumbled.

"Don't you feel afraid?" said Gargoylemog.

"I'm friendly to him so he's the same to me. Right, Argus, my man?"

As the dog's tail swept from side to side like a scythe, Gargoylemog shot Shane a strange look then waved him to follow.

***

After a winding downhill march they arrived at a wide glass door set into an almost perpendicular cliff. Before crossing the entrance, Gargoylemog said, "Know you anything about fish?"

Shane hesitated. "I used to fish a lot in Oz but…" He fell silent.

"And?"

"I'm not sure about killing fish anymore because…" He faltered as if embarrassed or unsure of what he wished to say. "When I see fish in the supermarket their eyes are always sad and open as if… well… they're trying to tell me something… know what I mean?" He looked up at Gargoylemog, expecting a response. The young Cyclops remained impassive, his eye focused unerringly on Shane's face as he pushed open the door.

Shane thought that his capacity to be surprised or overwhelmed by the Fomorian world had been exhausted. He was wrong. He was standing inside the most mind-boggingly expansive aquarium he could ever have imagined. Stretching into the distance and brightly lit from roof and floor, both sides of the main passageway comprised tall, perpendicular windows, each fronting separate waterworlds beyond.

"By using the correct balance of plant life and plankton," said Gargoylemog, "I ensure each individual section forms its own separate – what do you Up-Worlders call it – ecosystem?"

Nose pressed against glass, Shane was already hooked on the different variety of species swimming in and out of view. Above his head, multicoloured jellyfish slowly danced and trampolined in the water column. "So many lovely things," he whispered.

"You are looking at twenty-one different fish species – many endangered or extinct. We breed them here before they are fished out. Your Up-World science knows much about fish; what use is that when the fish are gone, eh? Perhaps when you realise your stupidity, *we* may be able to reintroduce them. Here are warm-water groups heated by our geysers; the long cavern ahead holds those from the colder oceans."

A wide swirl on the surface of the pool close by caught Shane's attention. "What's that, Garg?

"Shark, two immature Great Whites. I keep them apart. They take many years to mature and I feed them on sickly fish from other sections."

"Sick fish? Isn't that sort of cruel?"

"No cruelty, stupid," Gargoylemog snapped, his eye blinking erratically. "No hours of agony snagged in trawler nets or impaled on hooks. The Great White kills instantly."

From nowhere, the memory of his hooking the big fish on Granddad's beach hit Shane. "What about sea bass then?"

"They're in Section 5. Their numbers dwindle; I fear for them. There is something else you should see."

Gargoylemog led the way up one of the narrow stairways that separated each section of the aquarium. Shane watched the mesmeric collections of vivid corals that layered the bottoms, conscious for the first time in his life of just how beautiful the creatures of the ocean really were.

Gargoylemog pointed to the long adjoining expanse of calm water, devoid of obvious fish life. Partially illuminated by underwater lighting, Shane could still see no sign of activity except for the fronds of gently-waving seaweeds. "Not much going on down there, eh, Garg?"

Gargoylemog's eye closed in a knowing wink. "Wait here," he said, walking towards the long wooden board that stretched out over the water.

Reminds me of the high-dive platform back in Brisbane High; he's not going to jump, is he?

The plank trembled under Gargoylemog's weight as he shuffled towards the end where a sheet of tarpaulin lay, covering the body of a large seal, ropes loosely lashed around its tail. He blew three blasts on his whistle, then lay on his stomach, suspending the carcass over the water. His dangling arms took the weight of the animal's body, allowing it to hang free.

Nothing happened for a full ten seconds.

Shane heard the rumble before he saw anything. Below, the water boiled with sudden ferocity and the gigantic shape that erupted almost made his pulse stop. Nose first, like a sky-bound rocket, a shark shot upwards, a blur of yellow and brown-spotted muscle, its mouth widening, its body quivering. But it was the monstrosity's bulk that made Shane's brain spin – it was longer than the St Columbanus' school bus. By the time the open mouth had reached the seal, it had spread wide enough to encompass the height of a grown man. Gargoylemog released the seal into the cavernous jaws and the shark dropped tail-first, back into the pool in a further explosion of foam.

This is beyond dreams, beyond nightmares.

Continuing to stare with numb astonishment into the restless waters, he heard Gargoylemog holler, "What do you think of *that*, Up-Worlder?"

Shane tried to say something but no words came.

Gargoylemog's mischievous smile had grown even wider. "That," he said nonchalantly, "was a *Carcharodon megalodon.*"

"A *what*?"

"The largest ocean predator ever. From the Jurassic Period."

"Millions of years old? Come on? How can something that size still be around?"

"I shall explain all about Carca later. First, she has a big appetite." He pointed to a barrel overflowing with mackerel that sat on the jetty and removed the whistle from around his neck. "She's hungry. Three blasts, call her."

As he handed over the whistle, Gargoylemog frowned, then grabbed Shane's hand. "What is that?" he said, pointing.

"My Dad's ring. Why?"

As Gargoylemog bent closer, Shane saw the colour drain from his face. "What's wrong?"

"Why haven't you shown this to Homer?"

"I didn't think he'd…"

"…You fool, you absolute fool… *you didn't think?*"

"What's wrong?"

But Gargoylemog was already running towards the exit. "Hurry. Follow me," he shouted over his shoulder.

Chapter 29

Holding Shane's palm with both hands, the Bard looked older and more lined as his fingers ran over the Shane's ring.

"What's the problem, Homer?"

Shane had never paid any attention to the tiny inscriptions on his ring. For the first time he realised just what an unusual object the gold band really was. Somewhere within the depths of the gem centerpiece he could see three circles of gold, looped together. One second the coils glowed in clear focus, next they shimmered, almost vanishing from sight.

Homer again massaged the ring with his long fingers, then, to Shane's surprise, slipped it effortlessly off. Placing it on the nearby table, he began to crisscross the palm of his right hand over it many times, eyes shut, face rapt, as if feeling for some invisible stimuli emanating outwards.

"How long have you been wearing this?" he asked, his voice low.

"Well... for as long as I can remember..."

"...Didn't you think it strange that it might need adjustment as your finger grew? Was it ever tampered with or...?"

"...Not that I can remember, I..."

"...My fingertips detect faded letters. The etchings on shanks I cannot yet decipher." He set down the ring. "This is *Eochu's Ring of Power.*"

A gasp went up from the surrounding Cyclopes, followed by a murmur of excitement.

"So?" said Shane, glancing around uneasily.

Homer stared sightlessly into the distance, seeking the right words before replying. "I have insufficient time to sit you in the Seat of History so pay attention… thousands of years ago, Eochu imbued three rings with magical properties to protect our early civilisation from rampant evil. They were the rings of *CUMHACT*, meaning Power, *LEIGHEAS*, meaning Healing and *AITEAMH*, Persuasion."

"But what could they *do*?"

"We still know little about the Ring of Power; all we have are stories, myths and fanciful exaggerations. But, whosoever wore the Healing Ring could heal any laceration or wound. If somebody wore the Ring of Persuasion, then whoever was addressed immediately carried out the speaker's commands."

The recent memories of his trial came flooding back to hit Shane like a fist. *So that's how Indech got the crowd to depose King Tethra – he was using the Persuasion Ring!*

"Each ring carries unknown potency," continued Homer, "but two worn together would bestow great powers on the wearer. Possession of all three would confer, well, near invincibility."

"But, what happened to them?"

"The Tuatha de Dannan stole the Healing Ring from King Balor before the Battle of Moytura which enabled their army to turn out unblemished for battle while we retained gaping injuries. Balor's wife, Ceithlinn, gave the other two to King Tethra before she escaped to Inis Ceithlinn – today called Enniskillen."

Shane's mind was reeling. "So I've, I've been wearing the Ring of Power all my life and…?"

"…I was Bres' tutor. A brilliant headstrong student and a great athlete, he detested Indech. He eloped one day without warning but later returned with his wife and child. Only myself, Bres and his wife knew of this baby's existence. After murdering your parents, Indech sent Polyphemog to kill the only person who would stand between himself and eventual power – me – the king's trusted advisor. Polyphemog caught me departing to approach an Up-World family who might adopt Bres' newborn. I was carrying only toys and gold for the child's upbringing but I, er, *persuaded*, shall we say, Polyphemog to spare my life. He agreed only on condition that the child's existence, and mine, remained secret."

The uneasy stillness was broken by Shane's whisper. "The child you handed over to the Donnegans – was *me!*?"

Homer's reply was almost inaudible. "That you could be Bres' child was initially too bizarre for me to contemplate." He inhaled deeply. "But there can be no doubt, you are the boy I gave over for adoption, the son of Bres, grandson of King Tethra."

"You included *this* ring with my, my *toys*?"

"Something for you to remember your parents by."

In that awful hush, Shane stood stock still. *Everything now makes sense, well, some sort of sense...*

Homer slipped the ring back on Shane's finger. "Indech will stop at nothing to get that. Your presence has placed everyone in the Catacombs in the greatest danger…"

"Homer!"

Shane swung around towards the sound. The loud cry had come from a side opening as a Cyclops staggered into the torchlight. His bloody face covered in sweat and dust, he was barely able to stand. His right arm dangled at an unnatural angle.

"What has happened, Marlog?" called Homer.

181

"Indech with many soldiers. Four men and three hounds are dead. I came as quick as I could. Less than an hour's march."

Homer faced Shane. "You have ample time to make low tide at the Scaen Gate; depart now. We cannot protect you with spoons and quills. Eels, turtles and mastiffs cannot hold out against Indech. We have long feared this day."

Elatha interrupted. "Indech will have the Gates guarded, Homer. Is there another escape route?"

"One."

"Where?" chorused Shane and Elatha.

"A short distance from where you entered the Catacombs lie two tunnels; they are marked on your map. One carries solid waste, the other, wastewater. By dropping into a long, narrow cave, this water chute eventually opens to the sea, some distance beyond. Then it is a prodigious swim to the surface. Only one man ever completed it."

"Who?"

"Your father, Bres, our all-time swimming champion. But dismiss any thought of taking that route; your only hope is to plunge deeper into the uncharted caves…"

"…Let us depart, Shay-An," cried Elatha, vigorously tugging Shane's sleeve.

"Leave it out, Elatha," he snapped. "Homer, maybe I could get out by that wastewater tunnel?"

"No! That is well-nigh impossible. Malinmog will take you away from here, into Darkest Regions where Indech will never go. You will have to travel awhile in a deep, cold river; Malinmog will provide you with the necessary fat-cover for the swim."

"What will happen to you and your people, Homer?"

"They are *our* people. End this conversation now by taking your leave…"

"…Then I can't go, Homer. I'm responsible for Indech's coming. I can't leave you like this. I'm going to stay and fight…"

Homer's gnarled hand grabbed Shane. "Depart! Firstly you are too young and secondly you are no use to anyone dead. But, you might play a part in our future. So go. Go!"

"*Please*, Shay-An," pleaded Elatha again.

Distraught at the thought of letting Homer down, Shane glanced around for the last time, knowing that no matter what happened, he'd never meet such kind, helpful people again. In the dim light outside the communal hall and watched by the gathering of apprehensive Cyclopes, he and Homer shook hands, Up-World fashion. Although he tried to avoid looking at Homer's ravaged face, Shane was aware of the current of respect and understanding passing between them, experiencing for the first time an emotion he had read about somewhere – that mysterious chemistry which often bonds men together in extreme situations.

"Perhaps, Shane," whispered Homer, "you might return one day?"

"I…I…"

"Yes, maybe, one day…"

Shane realised that Homer knew this was their final goodbye – they would never meet again. In the short ensuing hush, he felt Homer place his left hand over their joined right hands and saw his own troubled face reflected in Homer's sorrowful eye. Despite his bursting heart, at that moment he knew there was nothing he could do or say to the Bard that might remotely express how he felt.

I want to thank him for… for so many things… But the words stuck in his throat. "Goodbye… thank you…" was all he could mutter and even that, with difficulty.

Homer released his grip and gesticulated towards the exit.

Slinging his bag across his shoulder, Shane sprang forwards, blindly beckoning Elatha and Malinmog to follow.

After a silent ten-minute jog, Malinmog called a halt at a gloomy T-junction where they briefly rested. He pointed. "Left to the deepest caves. Go."

"What's to the right?" said Shane.

"The wastewater tunnel. Here, take your seal fat," he said, roughly tossing over a leather pouch. "The River Styx is ice cold."

"Thanks, Malinmog, you've been very…"

Malinmog pressed his nose close to Shane's and grunted, "You are nothing but trouble." Before taking off at speed he added, "I hope Indech catches you both."

At a loss at what to say or think, Shane stared dumbly at the Cyclops' departing back until it was lost in shadow.

"What did Malinmog say?" asked Elatha.

"Oh, er, just saying goodbye. Come on."

"It is this way, Shay-An…"

"…No, I'm swimming out by the wastewater chute."

"You certainly are not!" she said, snapping to attention, her eyes burning.

Shane caught her by the wrist. "No arguments, Elatha," he said, his voice low and neutral. "This way."

***

Ten minutes later, Shane heard the first bloodcurdling shrieks in the deep distance and felt Elatha's nails gouge his arm.

"Indech," they mouthed together, exchanging wild looks.

Shane knew that sound travels long and fast underground, so as the remote rumblings grew in intensity, they bounced and ricocheted off the labyrinth's walls. Each reverberation chilled him to the marrow.

Elatha leant against a rocky outcrop to steady herself. "What's he *doing* to those poor people?"

"There's nothing *we* can do. Indech hasn't come all this way to tell me I've missed the last ferry. Keep moving."

Breaking into an even faster trot, Shane was unable to block out the heart-rending screams dogging their footsteps, stomach-churning cries that went on and on.

Chapter 30

How long it took to navigate the bridge and retrace their arduous journey Shane was unable to guess.

Lathered in perspiration and grime and almost dropping from exhaustion, they negotiated the limestone wall marking the entrance to the Catacombs. They scaled the intervening hazards and scurried along the narrow track leading to the volcano vents. Stopping to catch his breath, Shane advanced to peer into the gorge. The heat and sulphurous gases hitting the back of his throat made him splutter, then stumble.

"I can't face that, Elatha. Not in a million years."

She put an arm around his waist and ran her fingertips gently over his face. "There is no other way, Shay-An," she whispered, a catch in her voice.

"Some choice. It's either this…or that madman behind us." His jaw tightened. "Which tunnel leads to the outside?"

Elatha pointed at the shrivelled remnants of vegetable peelings and fish heads. "That leads to the volcano so the other must end up in..."

As if to confirm what she'd said, a long rush of water sounded somewhere in the darkness above, then struck the nearby wall. It careered downwards into the nearest chute, showering them with foul-smelling effluent.

"Ugh," Shane gasped. "So I have to go down with all that poo stuff?"

"Please advance to the ledge."

A familiar voice from behind froze Shane's blood. "I think not."

They swung around and there in the shadows stood Indech, arms folded, smiling triumphantly, the Locator-Max at his feet. In his eyes there was nothing, no expression, only a shimmering inky brilliance. As Shane checked for the presence of soldiers or Cyclopes, Indech's sneering words cut through his thoughts.

"Just me. Certain tasks are best carried out alone. I shall not use my ring to persuade you; no, I will crush you with my bare hands. As for you, traitor daughter of a traitor, I shall settle my account with you later."

As he approached, and without looking at Elatha, he nonchalantly slashed a thin-bladed knife across her tunic, opening a long gash across her left arm. She screamed and fell to her knees, sobbing with desperate abandon, attempting to stem the flow of blood with the loose strip of cloth that dangled from the garment. Shane, trying to get his head around this display of wanton violence, grasped one of the daggers in the rear of his belt, commanding himself not to lose his cool.

I have to use these weapons. No choice. We're both dead unless I fight my corner.

In one smooth movement, he manoeuvred the whale-bone handle free, index and middle fingers positioned along the shaft. Perfectly balanced for throwing. He could hear his teeth chattering as he slid the weapon clear of his belt.

Indech was four metres away when Shane arched his arm backwards and with weight evenly distributed on both feet, launched the knife with as much accuracy and venom as he could muster. Neither Indech's demeanour nor gait changed as he casually took the full impact on the chest, where the knife bounced off harmlessly with a hollow clang. His smile grew smugger.

"Body armour," he said conversationally, throwing back his cloak to expose the engraved metal breastplate underneath.

Shane drew the second dagger, undecided about his next move; throw or fight hand to hand? Neither option filled him with optimism.

"Fancy your chances? Pampered brat versus a Fomorian warrior?" sneered Indech. "Pah!"

Tossing aside his body armour and habit, Indech drew himself to full height, clad only in a loincloth, sandals and knee-high stockings. From his lean frame, taut muscles protruded that Shane knew could only have resulted from a daily discipline of workouts and a tough diet.

Hoping to catch him off guard, Shane lunged. With hardly any effort, the druid ghosted past like a skilled footballer avoiding a clumsy tackle.

"Too impetuous, half-breed," he said, wagging a finger.

Indech shimmied left, right, then grabbed Shane's wrist, pinning him against a boulder. Drawing his blade along the lower jaw, he barely pierced skin but opened up a superficial wound then flung Shane aside. "First blood," he sneered. "You have a long and painful route ahead, which I shall greatly enjoy."

Stumbling on hands and knees, Shane spat a mixture of dust and saliva, frantically scanning the ground for some other weapon – a sharpened stick, a brick, anything. But there were none. A sudden explosion of pain erupted as Indech drove his knee into Shane's ribs, pitching him over and over. He distinctly heard the crunch of his skull bones as he struck the cavern wall, trying to squint through his dizziness.

I'm hurting everywhere. Another blow like that and I'm finished. Is this how you feel when you are going to die?

He shook his head, flicking away droplets of perspiration and clearing his brain of any thought of defeat. He watched Indech raise his arm. *I'm totally in the open, unprotected...and he's going to throw a knife...*

Instinctively Shane bent his knees and went into an automatic squat. As Indech launched his weapon, Shane, using every erg of energy, suddenly launched himself into a well-practised backflip. As his feet hit the ground, he heard the dagger ricochet off rock somewhere behind.

"Very good footwork," mocked Indech, as he darted forwards to retrieve the weapon. Replacing it in his belt he added, "Did you hear Homer and his choir crooning their merry, tongueless tunes? Thank you for helping me clear out that wasp nest of savages."

Shane used his raised arms to fend off the next onslaught but Indech cavorted from side to side, weaving and bobbing as he launched a blurred flurry of blows that sent Shane tumbling to the ground.

He doesn't want to stab me − yet. Those bangs to the head are the worst. Everything is getting dim. Is my eye beginning to close...?

Scrambling on all fours, he was desperately trying to hold on to his consciousness but Indech caught him from behind, viciously wrenching him by the hair. Mouth against Shane's ear, he grated, "I killed your parents *and* your grandfather. You are the last of that squalid line of traitors."

From nowhere Shane saw Elatha's tear-stained face appear from the shadows, approaching Indech from behind. A rock held above her head, she brought it down in a vicious arc.

But, out of the corner of his eye, the druid had been alerted by some slight movement. With a snakelike turn of speed, he twisted aside as Elatha's missile descended, missing his head and barely grazing his shoulder. In almost the same movement, he landed a punch to Elatha's temple, knocking her to the ground where she knelt, holding her head in both hands.

"Use your ring, Shay-An," she wept. "Oh, use your ring."

Indech contemptuously spat at the forlorn figure then drove her to the ground with a kick into the small of her back. He removed the knife from his belt and with the weapon extended, turned to Shane.

"Hand here, mongrel. Accept the removal of your finger. That ring is mine. Mine!"

"Whatever you say, sir," mumbled Shane, bowing his head.

Indech's eyes glittered with sly triumph. He exhaled slowly and almost smiled.

A costly mistake.

Too intent on his prize, Indech had failed to see Shane's left foot sweeping along the ground before it smashed against Indech's ankle, knocking him off balance. Shane's follow-up blow to the chest had little effect, but the second punch from his ringed hand was different. The druid's forehead jerked back as if he had been struck by a log. Another dull thud sounded against his temple. Scrupulously following Sensei Tanaka's karate routines, Shane drove Indech further back with each advancing, alternating strike. He could feel the ring's pulsations grow stronger.

As his back hit the cavern wall, the groggy Fomorian leader raised and aimed his ringed finger. Shane had no time to avoid the emissions of what appeared to be tiny dots of green tracer emanating from the ring. Everything went limp as his energy drained away.

"Amputation time, hybrid. Hand."

Shane forbade his limbs to respond but some uncanny power was forcing his elbow up. He watched, trance-like, as if with a will of its own, his arm continued to extend towards Indech. "No," he choked.

He felt his hand begin to itch, as if his ring was somehow burning his skin. *It's glowing purple – yes, that's it! My ring must've stopped me being affected by Indech's commands in the courtroom. I must use it somehow; my last hope. Concentrate... it only responds when I really concentrate... I have to order it to work for me...*

As he squeezed his eyes shut, without warning, power began to sizzle back into his muscles, allowing him to turn and aim his ring at Indech. Only three metres apart, the panting pair grimly eyeballed one another, shuffling in a tight circle, arms extended, ring fingers outstretched. Shane was using his every fibre to fight against whatever force was pushing against his torso and limbs, against his very brain. Each of the rings' pulsations attracted the other, yet on intersecting, they dissipated into multicoloured motes of light. Lurching back from the invisible onslaught, Shane felt his energy wane again.

How can I block the Ring of Persuasion's powers? I wish I understood my own ring's...

Abruptly, Indech's fingers were around his throat.

"Face into the ground, scum. See what crossing me brings you. You will learn the hard way, like your father before you. As will Connaing's young bitch." He turned, pointed his ring and shouted, "Disobedient daughter of a renegade; get yourself to the edge and throw yourself over."

Smiling through bloodied lips, Indech brought his forehead close to Shane's, their sweat intermingling. "Enjoy watching your vixen taking her last steps," he rasped. "Then it's your turn."

Indech was savouring Elatha's zombie-like progress towards the gorge when Shane again felt a flow of fresh energy surge through his muscles. Enveloped by Indech's arms, he was unable to move his lower body so he whipped his head back and in almost the same movement, snapped it forwards, crashing his forehead into the bridge of Indech's nose. As the druid staggered and attempted to regain his composure, Shane was back on his feet. He slammed the sole of his foot into Indech's flat belly and saw the silver gleam of fear and incredulity flash somewhere within the druid's eyes. Exhaling violently with blood running down his nose, Indech staggered backwards, arms flailing, trying to regain his balance. Close to the edge as his feet scrabbled to gain a foothold, he steadied himself sufficiently to reach the knee-high stocking of his right leg. In a nimble movement he'd exposed the sheath strapped to his calf. With an audible grunt of satisfaction, he whipped the long dagger free, its tip pointing at Shane.

"I won't just kill you, I will eat your liver," he said softly.

With cold certainty, Shane knew that the next few moments would separate winner from loser… *But if he gets away from the edge, I'm dead.*

Without hesitation he leapt forwards as Indech lunged to drive the blade into his entrails. In a smooth-flowing series of distractory movements, Shane took two backward steps then suddenly balanced his weight on his left leg and angled his body backwards. Assuming Shane had lost his balance, Indech leapt forward, snarling like a dog. Shane cocked his right leg then snapped it forward, powerfully driving his heel into oncoming Indech's kneecap. He never knew whether the audible crack came from splintering bone or a snapping tendon, but Indech had collapsed to one knee, half kneeling, half standing, but still grasping the dagger.

Shane flicked the sweat from his eyes. "A nice Hiza Geri," he panted

He took a further step forward and coldly delivered a full-blooded kick into Indech's solar plexus that propelled him back to the rim of the gorge. Shane advanced like a matador preparing to deliver the final sword thrust to the bull's heart and as Indech struggled to remain upright, he contemptuously pushed him over the edge. He coldly watched the druid spiral out of sight.

"For my Mum and Dad," he said coldly, "And for Granddad and Homer and the..."

Elatha!

He swung around to see her approaching the edge of the void. Aiming his ring, he hollered, "Stop, Elatha. Stop!"

Dreamlike, she halted in mid step and remained motionless, blinking erratically. He sprinted to her side and cradled her haggard face. "Elatha, Elatha. Are you OK?"

"I will see you in the next world, Shay-An…"

"…Snap out of it," he said, gently caressing both sides of her face with his palms. "Please, come back to me, Elatha, please…"

Her vacant eyes widened then flared with recognition. "Oh, Shay-An, it was horrible, horrible. I remember thinking that I did not want to do it but that if I did, then all would be right."

"Let me see what that creature did to your face."

He scanned her jaw and temple, relieved to see the flesh was unbroken, only bruised. Still trying to dismiss the sound of Indech's body bouncing off rock, he knew he should be feeling guilt, or some kind of remorse but was only aware of being glad it was all over.

"But Shay-An, how did you stop me from…?" She sobbed and didn't continue.

"...The Ring of Power," he said, staring down at Eochu's still-pulsating ring.

He saw her eyes widen as she scanned his battered body and ragged, bloodied appearance. *I can still feel electricity surging through my veins... my muscles are still twitching like anything. I hope I didn't appear too much of a savage; I had no choice....*

"You were terribly brave, Shay-An, I thought ..."

"...So were you, Elatha; trying to take out Indech like..."

"...Why keep staring into the gorge, Shay-An?"

"I've gotta be sure Indech's gone for good."

"Do not be stupid, nobody could survive that fall. You resembled an animal, a beast, do you know that? But you saved me." She gently ran her fingers through his matted hair. "Please change back to the Shay-An I knew."

His fierce expression didn't change but as their eyes locked, his breathing slowed, the aggression began to subside. He unconsciously stroked her face as he kicked the miodóg over the precipice.

"Me, I'm really bushed," he sighed, arms dropping by his sides. "I don't think I can face the long swim."

"You have no choice."

Chapter 31

He washed and cleaned her laceration, then rebound the makeshift bandage over the gaping wound.

"I'm sure it needs stitches and that but at least I've stopped the bleeding." Becoming aware of how she looked, he added, "You look all in."

She glanced at his tattered, filthy clothes and hair stiff with grime and blood then smiled wanly. "Have regard to your own appearance, Mister Shay-An."

He wasn't thinking clearly and hadn't got around to asking her but he was somehow hoping she might think of accompanying him back to the outside world. *Maybe just for a quick visit or something?* Now that the pounding in his ears was subsiding, the rest of his life was limping back into focus. *How would she take to it; cars, computer games and those shops and discos she fancied? Come to think of it, she probably knows as much about discos as I do.*

Elatha must have known what was on his mind. "You comprehend that I can never depart from here? This is my home; the Up-World is your home."

"But why not, Elatha? Maybe those councillor guys would let you out for a break with me? After all, I am one of you. For a picnic? Maybe get special permission, you know, like a day pass or something? What about us applying to become apprentice Watchers or something? I live in Westport, not exactly a million miles away. You can bring back things your people need; like medicines and clothes. Maybe you might fancy trying out those chocolates and pizzas I was telling you about…"

"…No, Shay-An," she said, placing her finger on his lips, "this is my home. Perchance you consider us different, believing in things at odds with what you do. But we Fomorians are like the sea anemone, which lies dead and exhausted on the rocks at low tide, but flowers into strange and lively colours when water flows over it once more. We have no need of your many *things* – the cars and the mac donalds. Until Indech began his drive for power, we had contentment here. We lived for ourselves and each new day. I must find out if my parents are dead or…no, I cannot go. Perhaps one day you might retrace your steps here; to visit me? Maybe if we are really desperate for Up-World things?"

He could already feel the start of a lump in his throat. "I'm a Fomorian, Elatha. Your secrets are mine but I've got to get back to Dad and my friends. They'll be worried sick. But I don't want to lose you…"

"…Shay-An, our society is in chaos. It is dangerous to tarry. Many angry men here don't laugh and joke like you; they fear and detest the Up-World. It is my fondest wish that you should remain here but you must depart. Now. Lugh will be looking for you as will Indech's son…"

"…What?" he gasped. "Indech had a son?"

"Indech-the-Younger, he's just like his father. They all want you dead. Enough; quickly smear yourself with fat then get on to the ledge."

"It'll be pitch dark down there, Elatha; I'll never be able to see where I'm…"

"…Shay-An, every Fomorian can see clearly underwater and with practice, see in the dark. We retain this facility from birth. Remember, concentrate and be patient."

The stillness was oppressive as they moved reluctantly towards the wastewater chute, arms around each other's waists. Neither wanted the other to leave. But there could be no other way. Reaching the threshold, Elatha held him tightly, cheek against cheek, unable to speak. Shane could feel tears not far away. He remained motionless on the ledge, trying to fight down his inner turmoil, knowing that his life depended on his swimming ability, nothing else.

He stepped on to the ledge at the top of the chute and tore off his clothes, leaving only his jeans in place. Regretfully he slipped off his best trainers. "As little weight as possible," he explained needlessly. Next he removed his mobile and torch and checked that both were working. "I'm amazed they survived," he muttered. "You keep these, the salt water will screw them up anyway. Maybe I could ring you and another thing I…"

"…Converse no more. It is time."

His lips trembled as he put his own hand up to hold hers. Neither of them would look at each other, they were confused and brimming with an emotion neither could understand or explain. For those few moments there was nothing around them but silent stillness, as if everything in the Fomorian underworld, even the rocks, was holding its breath.

Elatha withdrew her fingers and placing both palms on his nape, said softly, "Inhale deeply." Although she tried to keep her voice calm, her face betrayed her. "Remember, I will always be thinking of you. Listen for me in the summer evenings – when you hear the leaves sigh in the trees and there is no wind, it will be me, whispering to you."

I know leaves can't rustle without wind but I don't care one little bit, I'll still be listening, clutching your stones, waiting…

Elatha's voice rose as she fought back her tears, trying to find the right words. "Goodbye, goodbye, Shay-An."

In the eerie volcanic glow, he saw her bright hair, her lovely, vivid face and her melting gaze for the last time.

He checked his watch. He would always remember that place, remember that time: 9.52. He could feel himself starting to shake and desperately wanted to convey his troubled feelings as she bent down and kissed him. Then, pushing hard against the muscles of his back, she launched him down the chute.

"Goodbye, Elatha, oh, I wish…" were his last words as his weight took him along the steep incline, whizzing over the smooth wet surface as hot air and stinking gases pressed against his eyeballs and rushed into his ears and nose. Teeth clenched, he could feel his speed increasing, aware of the fast approaching drop that would take him away from that unique and sweet someone he'd only known for such a short time. Someone he could never forget, no matter how long he lived…

Chapter 32

Still trying to estimate how long it would take to hit the water, he felt the change in his downward momentum. The shaft was losing some of its steepness, levelling out or coming to some sort of shelf...

The seat of my jeans is giving way; I can feel blisters popping over my back from the heat; the drop must come soon...

The darkness was near total as he inhaled the longest and deepest breath he'd ever taken. There was nothing beneath his legs and he fell into an emptiness, frantically trying to find footholds that weren't there. He seemed to hang forever in the black void before he crashed into water with a resounding smack, trying to fight his increasing panic.

Concentrate! Unless I get everything right from step one, I'll drown. Real quick. Which direction do I take?

By commanding himself to relax and remain motionless, he felt the drag of the current against his legs then opened his eyes. YES! I can see clearly! *At least the tide's taking me out towards the open sea... that'll speed me up a little...*

But the questions bouncing inside his head wouldn't go away. *How wide's this shaft? Any dead ends leading off? What if there's a fork somewhere and I take a wrong turning? What if...? Too many what ifs... Concentrate... Patience...* He shut out all extraneous thoughts and ordered himself to focus solely on the swim, aware that the roof was grazing his scalp while his fingers and toes were able to touch the sides and bottom of the tunnel. His watch's luminous dial said 9.54.

Two minutes gone.

His hand bumped against something drifting close by – a mass of hair, matted with pieces of shattered skull and brain tissue. He involuntarily recoiled and jerked away from the horror. King Tethra's lifeless face showed whitely as his bloated body bobbed past.

Indech must've chucked poor Granddad down the waste chute like a pile of garbage...

He steeled himself to overcome the urge to vomit, frantically using the clarity of Tethra's murder to drive him onwards to where the waterway divided into two. *Which one do I take?* His immediate choice was to take the broader, deeper channel to the right but something made him hesitate. He momentarily stopped swimming and floating high in the water, allowed the current to drag his left and right arms towards the different openings. *The right tunnel feels warmer! The cold draught blowing through the left means there must be oxygen coming from somewhere. Air!*

Fervently hoping he'd made the correct decision, he took the narrower option and felt the pressure inside his chest increase, as if someone was slowly tightening a powerful vice around his ribs. He dared not check the time again but it felt as if he'd been swimming forever. The pounding in his eardrums was becoming violent, the thudding inside his head almost unbearable. Then came the crushing realisation – *I'm not going to make it.* No longer able to control his bodily movements, he shot upwards, cracking his skull against rock and his mouth jerked open.

Instead of a rush of water, he was suddenly breathing air.

Air!

Panting and wheezing like an animal, he took in the claustrophobic surroundings. He'd surfaced into a con-cavity in the roof of the tunnel; a life-giving air-pocket. Pushing his upper body out of the water, he rested his elbows on the sides of the small grotto. At some considerable height above his head, a thin shaft of moonlight shone through a cleft in the surface of the island. *My sixth sense saved me again. Or was it my Fomorian genes...?*

And then he saw it, no further than a metre away – someone had scratched a single word on the ceiling: BRES. Another human being had somehow stumbled into the same miracle air hole – his father! *What a fantastic flukey coincidence! So that's how Bres had been able to make it to the Up-World. Getting out's impossible on a single lungful.*

Finding a sharp pebble, he scraped the words LORCAN - SHANE beside his father's name. He was ready to continue. *The no-mercy stretch,* he thought, sliding back into the current.

Time had now lost all meaning.

He passed rocky honeycombs and waving fronds which were becoming more distinct and as the tunnel became shallower, he just knew the ocean had to be very close. Without warning, an eel's head shot out from a nearby hollow, its jaws opening and closing menacingly. Recognising it as a conger eel, not a monstrous *eascann*, he swallowed his fear, knowing it only looked fearsome because it possessed no gills and that was its way of breathing. They seldom attacked humans unless provoked. To be bitten by one, you'd have to be daft enough to place a hand in its mouth.

It's the end of the tunnel. Faith's *echo sounder had registered a hundred metres depth around the island. Gotta hope this particular spot isn't that deep. Here goes...*

Wait. What did Tubs tell me about the bends? Ascend too fast and the nitrogen in your blood goes ballistic or something; you end up either in agony or with brain damage. No choice; I'll have to take my chances….

Using the sea floor to launch himself upwards, he shot for the surface, his exhausted air now escaping in desperate gulps. But he had nothing left to expel, the boundless ocean was pressurising his mouth to open. Flames of pain in every colour of the spectrum were sweeping through his body; the thought of being relieved of the thousands of piercing white hot needles was becoming more attractive by the second. *Just to sleep. To be done with it all.* He felt the first wash of water hit the back of his throat.

Then, in a technicolour flash, he saw Emelda, her face shining and clear, bending over his cradle, eyes glistening with love. In a blink, she had become Finnoula, singing a lullaby, her words soft and crystal clear;

"Go to sleep, my baby,

Close your big black eyes,

Angels up above you,

Peeping from the skies…"

Momentary glimpses of his early childhood began flicking past, each being quickly replaced by newer, more recent, vivid images of Brisbane, school…

This is what many drowning men experience – past episodes of their life flashing consecutively by in vivid detail. I'm going to die….

As water forced open his lips and swished around his teeth, the horror of his imminent death was suffused with the calming certainty of having seen his mothers. As he swallowed the first mouthful of seawater, he knew he had been loved by not one, but by two….

Chapter 33

Shane exploded into the open Atlantic, his oxygen-starved body shooting high out of the water. Gulping down life-giving air, he spluttered, coughing violently, trying to clear his throat and nose. Giddy and nauseous, he saw the reassuring bulk of the Island less than fifty metres away. Still quivering from the excess of adrenaline fizzing through his veins, he floated gratefully on his back, every nerve aware of the night, the heavens, the tang of the breeze.

That was so close!

10.09.

Over seventeen minutes – no way could I have made it without that air hole. Or without being able to see where I was going. My joints are free of pain – yippee – no bends either.

Behind, he heard a sigh, the sound of someone beyond hope or exasperation. Three metres away, a massive tail rose high out of the water, glistening ebony. His heart went into overdrive as the bulk almost touched his legs before noiselessly gliding below.

"A whale," he gasped.

Further away the great mammal resurfaced, its head turned, as if watching Shane. It noisily blew water through its spout and disappeared into the depths.

Maybe I conked out on the way up? Did that whale help me to the surface?

All around, the stars were reflected in the smooth, oily tide, shining as bright as in the sky, resembling millions of candles burning beneath the surface. He stared at the countless stiletto points of light piercing the night, somehow feeling close to them. For that split second, the enormity of existence hit him full on. The moment passed and he lay half-submerged, drinking in the thrill of just being alive.

So much has happened; time has lost all meaning; I need sleep...

Treading water, he promised himself he would be super-conscious of the smallest things that happened to him from that very moment onwards. His close contacts with death had been so vivid that he now wanted to squeeze the last drop of juice from every living experience. Burger and chips came to mind – with ketchup. Curry sauce maybe? And what about sending the goalie the wrong way when scoring from a penalty?

My teeth are chattering; Homer's seal fat won't keep out the cold for much longer. Exposure! I'd better get cracking for the shore...

"There he is!"

He recognised his Dad's voice! Nearby. And it sounded great. Some fifty metres away, the *Island Queen* had rounded the island, its searchlight sweeping the intervening stretch of sea, illuminating Shane's head and shoulders in magnesium-bright light. He waved furiously and hollered, "Here! I'm here!"

As the ferry drew closer, he could make out the figures of Tubs and Zara, gesticulating and pointing. Tubs was giving the thumbs up to everyone, grinning like a loon. Cheerful faces lined the rail while a burly policeman was punching the air with massive fists.

The engines of the red and black vessel cut to neutral as it drifted close, allowing a ladder to be lowered overboard. The aluminum structure bounced and sang as Shane scrambled upwards, helped aboard by numerous hands. Mr Donnegan grabbed his son and held him in a fierce embrace. Shane tried not to get pierced by the Brisbane Fishermen's Union badge jutting from his Dad's lapel.

Although the pair were surrounded by a wide knot of well-wishers and crew, only the soft throb of the diesels broke the silence during that long, uninterrupted hug.

"Great to see you… Dad."

Mr Donnegan's reply was almost inaudible. "Good to have you back, Shane." Seeing the injuries, he held his son at arm's length. "What's happened to your face?" he gasped.

Shane remembered Indech's attacks and how very close he'd been to never seeing his wonderful Up-World again.

"I'll explain everything later." His voice dropped so that only his father could hear their exchange. "I know about who I am and all that." Despite himself, a single tear flowed down each cheek.

"It's OK, son," Mr Donnegan whispered, also speaking with difficulty. "It's OK."

Tubs launched himself forward to break things up. "Great stuff, Shane," he cried, exchanging high fives.

Next Zara moved out of the circle of onlookers. "I love your dishy rigout," she said, pointing at Shane's tattered jeans and bleeding feet. "All the rage."

"How's it going yourself, Zara?" He could think of nothing else to say.

Sergeant Canny pushed to the fore. "Ahoy, young Donnegan," he chortled. "Begob, aren't ye the lucky young buck? Here's a change of clothes and what's that greasy muck all over you? And Jumping Jack, that kisser of yours looks like it stopped an articulated lorry." He clapped Shane heartily on the back. "There's two helicopters full of them reporters and TV people wanting to interview ye back in the hotel, face and all." He sauntered off, rubbing his hands together, leaving the three happy friends staring tearfully and happily at each other.

**

The following morning, Shane's meeting with the media in the hotel was unsatisfactory from a news point of view because he was determined to tell as little as possible about what had really happened in the caves. Despite being faced with TV cameras, a ring of bright lights and numerous reporters, his overriding concern was keeping Elatha and the Fomorians' existence a secret. *Play dumb,* he repeatedly reminded himself; *tell them nothing.* Because most of his answers and responses to the reporters' eager questions were simple *yeses, nos* or *I-can't-remember*s, the journalists quickly lost interest and folded their notebooks, concluding that Shane's memory had been somehow damaged by his ordeal. Before they left for the mainland, many gave Shane their business cards and requested a full report if and when he'd fully recovered.

On Clare Island's only road, Tubs and Zara moseyed on ahead toward *Faith's* mooring place. Shane and his Dad ambled behind, deep in conversation. They stopped, neither aware of the soaring skylark songs coming from the nearby fields.

"Shane, I know I missed your birthday but I was always wondering how I would explain everything to you…"

Shane tried to disguise his anger but didn't succeed. "That's a lame excuse," he grunted. "What stopped you telling me that you and Mam weren't my real folks?"

Unable to find the words, Mr Donnegan stared sightlessly ahead, running his fingers through his hair. "Don't be too hard on me, son," he said eventually. "Maybe I should've told you a long time ago, but how could I, my own memory was so confused? I knew you weren't my real son but I was mystified as to the reason – everything was murky, cloudy, like. Whenever I did pluck up the courage to discuss things with you, the words would stick in my craw because I didn't know how you'd react. It's only now that I understand I'd been hypnotised; I was in the dark myself for all these years and I was worried... worried... that you mightn't love me anymore." He coughed into his handkerchief. "I just didn't want to, to... lose you."

"You've always looked after me and loved me. I know that. So what if my real father was Bres? And my real mother was Emelda? No matter what happens, you will always be my Dad." He hesitated then said simply, "I love you, Paddy Donnegan."

It took some seconds before the reply tumbled out. "I love you too... Shane... my son." After a short silence he added, "It's probably best that all this is just between you and me; what do you think, son?"

"Sure, Dad."

Anyone taking a stroll by the harbour that early afternoon would have been surprised to see a man and a tall teenager hugging each other in the middle of the deserted road. They'd have seen the pair eventually separate then turn and walk contentedly towards the tethered boats, arms around each other's shoulders.

Chapter 34

Granddad's living room was alive with sunshine. Mr Donnegan was clearing breakfast things from the table, shaking his head in disbelief as Shane finished recounting another insignificant Fomorian incident.

Zara was inspecting her varnished fingernails. "Was Elatha really *that* beautiful, Shane?" she nonchalantly asked.

It was on the tip of his tongue to say something else, but Shane thought better of it. "Nah, she was just sort of OK, I suppose."

"How are we going to explain those scabs?" Mr Donnegan said for the nth time.

Although the bruising was beginning to change to a dirty yellow, Shane's facial skin was puffy and distorted, his lips mottled and scabbed.

"You'll have to tell a few teeny-weeny little porkies, Mr D," said Tubs with exaggerated seriousness.

"I don't like telling lies, Finbar, but sometimes it becomes necessary."

"You can't expect anyone to buy the truth either, Mr Donnegan," said Zara. "What happened to down there sounds like something from a sci-fi movie..."

"...A horror movie," said Tubs, giving one of his customary squeals.

"Those scabs," said Zara, "should be well healed by the new term."

Tubs caught Mr Donnegan's sleeve as he passed. "You're in denial about Shane," he said with mock seriousness. "Your son's really a ravin', demented psycho who'll stop at nothin'."

Mr Donnegan frowned. "Finbar, we've all agreed that whatever took place down there does not go beyond the confines of this here cottage, is that understood? When he gets his full memory back, Shane will be able to tell us what *really* happened. We've all seen what those post-hypnotic suggestions can do."

"What about the ring?" said Tubs.

Mr Donnegan theatrically dropped a handful of cutlery on the table. "I'm convinced much about that ring is more post-hypnotic gobbledygook. Like normal people, let's now have a proper holiday by which time, according to Dr Grimes, Shane should be back to his old self. In the meantime, let's hide that ring somewhere out of harm's way."

"Where?" said Zara.

"Safest place in the world," Mr Donnegan replied, throwing them a know-all look. Enjoying the fact that he was finally getting one up on them for a change he added with a chuckle, "I thought you modern teenagers knew everything?"

"The eye," breathed Zara.

"Exactly. What do you think, Shane?"

"My ring stays with me."

Mr Donnegan coughed loudly. "Whose turn to wash up?" he asked, busying himself at the table, eager to change the subject.

"Hey, we're all on the telly!" cried Tubs, bounding towards the remote and bumping up the volume.

Household chores forgotten, the friends threw themselves onto the sofa to catch the tail end of *Breaking News Ireland.*

A view of Clare Island's harbour panned across the screen, followed by a brief clip of Shane, Zara and Tubs grinning and waving at the camera. The newscaster's voice cut in. *"The search for schoolboy, Shane Donnegan, believed drowned off Clare Island, had a happy ending when he was found alive and well last night. A rogue wave had earlier dragged him into an underwater cavern where there was sufficient oxygen to keep him alive. He lived on rainwater and raw shellfish and when sufficiently recovered, was able to swim back to the surface. Despite the young man being his school's swimming champion, local Gardaí say his survival is nothing short of miraculous."*

Zara waited until Mr Donnegan had retreated to the kitchen before standing up, hands on hips. "This pledge of secrecy," she announced, "will be very hard to keep, yeah?"

"I'd love to tell everyone," gushed Tubs, "but I get enough stick without wild stories. Maybe tell just a few friends, Shane?"

"We're the only ones," Shane said grimly, "who know about the Fomorians and we keep it that way. We trust nobody but ourselves. Dad won't say a thing but if word ever got out then bet your life that Amazon would soon be dropping off parcels down there. The Fomorians depend on us keeping schtum about everything. So, let's each of us hold our Fomorian coin in our hand..."

Tubs gleefully rubbed his palms together. "This gold piece must be worth a small packet..."

"Forget money," snapped Shane. He placed his right hand on the table, a Fomorian coin inside his closed fist. "Zara, put your coin in your hand and place it over mine; Tubs, you do the same over Zara's hand. Then close your eyes and together we silently promise to keep Clare Island's dark secret to ourselves."

Tubs exchanged a knowing glance with Zara. "Isn't this gettin' a bit overdramatic..." he began.

"Just do what he asks, Tubs," Zara said sweetly and together all three shut their eyes.

Zara was first to open hers. "Maybe someday, Shane," she ventured, "we might go down there; on a daytrip or something? Only the three of us mind."

Shane didn't answer. The brightness streaming into the room was so unlike the recent half-light of the underground world. The sky seemed composed of such an unreal blue that he half expected it to shatter and expose grey Fomorian rock lurking behind. He felt as if he had fled into a bunker deep inside himself and was peering out at the surrounding normality through a narrow slit. *I can't even tell Zara and Tubs what really happened down there – neither can I tell them about what being a Fomorian means, because, well, I haven't got to grips with all that... yet.*

Checking that the wind wasn't rustling the leaves outside, his fingers fondled Elatha's stones inside his pocket. He wondered whether there might come a time when he wouldn't think of her, wouldn't relive every moment they'd shared. Still trying to dismiss the multitude of questions and unpleasant possibilities that kept hounding him, he rose from the sofa and absent-mindedly switched off the TV. Without a backward glance he walked out, head bowed, heading for the beach. Alone.

.

INDEX